Leopard in the Grass

Sue Bates

Second printed edition 2015

The Bothy Publishing
Terreran Bothy
Main Street
Gartmore
Scotland
FK8 3RN

www.bothy-publishing.com
enquiries@bothy-publishing.com

cover design by Judy Bullard/
www.customebookcovers.com/photograph courtesy of EPA
Sense of Wonder contest

ISBN 978-0-9929124-2-0

For family and friends of every species

Of course, I was amazed, when I saw a leopard hiding in the long grass in my back garden – it's not the sort of thing you expect, first thing on a Monday morning. What to do next? It was obvious I shouldn't go up to it and try to pat it – anything like that was silly. Obviously silly.

But I really was tempted to go up to it and pat it. But I didn't. But I didn't do other obviously *sensible* things, either, like phoning the police, alerting the zoos, phoning the RSPCA, even warning my neighbours. I felt protective of its privacy. This was *my* leopard hiding in *my* back garden. So I went to work, as usual (but I thought about my leopard all day – couldn't get it out of my mind and couldn't wait to get home).

As soon as I got home, I rushed to the window and looked for my leopard. It was still there. Its greenish-golden eyes spotted me staring and I think it snarled at me. It was telling me I shouldn't have ignored it and, at least, should have fed it something. A rabbit? A deer? But I'm a vegetarian and can't bear the thought of such death and destruction. So was I going to let it starve to death in my garden? And, if I did, I'd get prosecuted for

1

cruelty, even though it wasn't my fault – I hadn't asked for a leopard to hide in the grass in MY back garden.

There was nothing for it but to feed it cat food, and nobody would ever in a million years guess it was for a leopard hiding in the grass. But I had to be very careful – the people near me know I don't have a cat and I couldn't risk them finding out I was buying cat food when I only have a dog. So I put my coat back on and drove off to the furthest away pet store.

I bought three huge bags of dried cat food and then realised that my leopard would need water to drink. It always says on the instructions, *Have a bowl of water nearby*, something like that. Here was a problem – a bowl would be useless for a leopard. Leopards are big. It would need something like a pondful of water!

I went back into the pet store and over to the fish and fish pond area and bought the largest plastic fish pond I could find. The shop assistant had to help me out to the car with it and it only just fitted in the back with the boot open. And here was yet another problem. My neighbours would spot me struggling to get it out of my car and offer to help carry it round to my back garden and then they'd probably get pounced on by my leopard and in all likelihood eaten!

So I decided to drive about until it was dark and under cover of darkness and with the fish pond hidden under a sheet, I'd drag it out of my car and round to my back garden. I suppose at this point I was beginning to have doubts – perhaps I should give all this up and notify the authorities – but I'm not the quitting type.

After two hours it was nearly dark, so I drove towards home and, as I got close to my house, I coasted to a stop and didn't slam my car door as I usually do. I went into the house and found an old sheet and crept round to the boot where I managed to slip half of the sheet under the pond and cover it up with the other half. Slowly, slowly, I started dragging the pond out, and was just about to try lowering it to the ground, when a voice behind me said, "Here let me help you with that," and a large, middle-aged man lifted it out. "Where d'you want it putting?"

"Oh thanks...here in the front garden...on the lawn will do," I said.

"No problem," he said as he put it on my front lawn. "If you need any more help, I live up the road. Just moved in to number seven."

"Thanks very much," I said closing the boot quietly.

When the man was well out of sight, I dragged the fish pond round to the back garden and peered through the garden gate. There was still enough light to see the dark shape of my leopard's head above the grass. First, I would have to feed him and then, when he was full and sleepy, I'd drag the fish pond into the garden, and, there'd be a slim chance he wouldn't eat me – I say *he* but I didn't really know if he was a *he* but it didn't seem right to keep calling him *it* when we were just getting to know each other.

I went back to the car and struggled into the house with one of the bags of cat food. But I didn't want my leopard to become too domesticated and think he was relying on me for food, so I put a whole load of the food into a bucket and quickly lifted the bucket over the back garden gate and ran away, so he wouldn't know it was me who'd fed him, and then I forced myself to make myself some dinner and eat it slowly in front of the telly. But all the time I was thinking about my leopard and just couldn't wait to see if he'd eaten anything.

Archie, he's my dog, was getting more and more suspicious and sitting by the back door, asking to go out. But if I let him out, I knew exactly what he'd do – he'd shoot straight up to the back garden gate and jump right over it and make a good meal for my leopard, as I'm fairly certain that leopards prefer live dog food to dried cat food.

I waited a whole hour, which seemed like a whole day, before I went to see if my leopard had eaten anything. By now, it was very dark. I approached the garden gate cautiously and suddenly realised that if Archie could jump right over the garden gate, and he was only a fifth the size of a leopard, then, my leopard certainly could – no problem! I should have realised this earlier, of course – it would have saved me a lot of trouble. But there was no point in going back now. I was almost at the gate when I heard it, the sound of bones crunching. I stood perfectly still with my heart beating loudly as a huge shadowy form leapt over the gate. I ducked and he landed on the other side of me. In a flash, I opened the gate, ran through my back garden, down the lane, along the main street and into my house by the front door.

Archie had a shocked look on his face when I slammed the door behind me in a total panic. I think it was then that he decided he didn't want to go out, after all.

Now was certainly the time to alert the authorities. It was dark and there was a leopard on the loose in the neighbourhood – he could be eating one of the teenagers who hang around the shop at this very moment! And, if he did eat a teenager, I would be blamed.

I put my coat on and went out into the night with my torch. First, I went to the front of the house and looked up and down the main street. Nothing. Next, I went through my back garden and into the lane and shone my torch down it. Nothing. Leopards are fast runners so he could be in the next village by now eating teenagers there! I heard a rustling sound behind me. Should I run or stand still? I did neither. Instead I jumped up on to the stone wall bordering the farmer's field and turned and saw two bright eyes staring up at me from under my garden hedge. I sighed with relief. My leopard wasn't eating teenagers and I was saved from being the person known as the one who was so stupid she never told anyone about the leopard in her garden until it was too late.

I edged my way along the wall until I was a safe distance away from my leopard, jumped off the wall and sprinted all the way back to my house and shot in through the front door again.

I flopped down in my favourite chair to recover and Archie came and sat next to me and gave me a look. The dramatic entrances by the front door were beginning to get to him and he was obviously worried about my sanity too and he had a point. I needed to think more clearly. Perhaps my leopard liked me and my garden and the crunching of bones was actually the crunching of cat food and, when he jumped over the gate, he wasn't out to eat me at all. I was completely exhausted by this time and fell asleep in the chair.

Me and Archie woke up early. I was stiff and cold from sleeping in the chair but Archie was full of get up and go and wanted to get outside and go into the garden. Now was the time to put him in the picture.

"There's a leopard in our garden. You have to stay by my side," I told him, sternly.

I think he already knows about my leopard because, if you're a dog, I'm pretty sure you can smell a leopard a mile away.

I held on tight to Archie's collar and we went to check if my leopard was still in the long grass. We crept up to the back gate and peered through it. There he was – we could just see the top of his head. Archie's nose was working overtime and all the fur on his back stood on end but he didn't bark or growl, which was a sign that either leopards aren't the natural enemy of dogs or Archie has a lot of common sense and prefers to work silently undercover.

We went back inside and had our breakfast, as normal, and afterwards went for a walk down the main street, which wasn't normal. We usually went through the back garden and down the lane but, when you've got a leopard living in your garden, you have to make adjustments. After our walk, I dropped Archie off at my mum's and drove to work.

When I arrived, my boss said, "You look rough, Lily."

"So would you if you had a leopard living in your garden," I said.

"A leopard! You always were quirky," he gave me a brief look of concern. "How you getting on with the project? Nearly finished?"

"Nearly finished," I lied.

*

At last it was time to go home. The first thing I did was look for my leopard and to my joy he was still there – he was snoozing in the long grass and the bucket was empty, which definitely meant he needed some water, as well as more cat food, and I'd have to act quickly before he woke up.

I crept through the gate and grabbed hold of the bucket and crept out again. I dragged the fish pond through the gate and a little way into the back garden and attached the garden hose to the outside tap and switched on the water. The water swooshed out and sprayed out in an arc into the garden and a few drops landed on him. He opened one eye but I took a chance and kept on filling up the fish pond. When he opened his other eye I ran back inside where Archie was waiting for me.

"Don't worry you're safe in here," I told him.

*

There's something about having a leopard living in your back garden that raises you above the common herd and, when I went to work the next day, it must have shown because several people said I looked different. And, when my boss asked me if I would put the report on his desk by the end of the day, I surprised myself by saying, "No I won't," and walked away without a second thought and straight out of the building and had a two hour lunch break, which he often did.

Surprisingly enough, he didn't say anything to me when I reappeared, just kept glancing at me now and again when he thought I wasn't looking, and he even went so far as to suggest I needed a holiday.

"That would be good," I replied. I'll have plenty of time to care for my leopard, I thought.

*

All that week I did my work to the best of my ability, in the circumstances, which meant I hardly did any work at all. In fact, I realised that the less work I did the better I was treated and I got long lunch breaks. My boss called me to his office and to my astonishment offered me twenty thousand pounds if I left at the end of the month with no recriminations. I said I'd consider it. Reward for failure they call it.

*

I got into a routine. I left work early and as soon as I got home, I checked if my leopard was still there, filled up the bucket with cat food, placed it over the back garden gate, filled the fish pond with water and then took Archie for a walk. This worked well for a whole week until my leopard must have got bored with lying in the long grass all day – and he was probably getting a bit chubby too, with all that lying about. I say *probably* because I never got a full view of him and I still didn't know if *he* was a *he* – all I'd seen was the glint of his eyes or the shifting of his beautiful spots through the long grass.

When I got home on that fateful day and checked if my leopard was still there, he wasn't! Archie set to work with his reliable nose tracking down my leopard, along the back lane and into the field. I was wearing my work clothes – high heels, black leggings, short skirt, jumper, bag slung over my shoulder – so I wasn't dressed for traipsing across fields, but there was no time to go back just when me and Archie were hot on the trail.

Eventually, we came to a stream, which threw Archie off the scent for a few seconds, and so, using my initiative, I attempted to leap across the stream and landed in the middle and got very wet and muddy. Meanwhile, Archie was across, without even getting his paws wet, and already hot on the trail on the other side. He's a much better leaper than me.

Across another field and another until we came to the next village, where I feared things could get very tricky. People were sure to get suspicious when they saw me covered in mud. They'd start asking questions and I wasn't convinced that saying I was tracking down my semi-domesticated leopard would go down too well.

The village shop was open so I dashed in, quickly bought two packets of biscuits and a bottle of water, and rushed back to Archie, who was waiting outside. But all Archie's attention was now centred on the biscuits and as far as he was concerned my leopard could do just what it liked.

"Ok, we'll eat a few biscuits," I said and walked out of the village and sat down on a bench overlooking the village school.

As I sat down, Archie started barking at a group of walkers coming round the corner and heading straight for us.

"Send'em off," I said under my breath to Archie, in the hope they'd think he was fierce and that would stop them getting too close and asking awkward questions.

It didn't work. They came right up to us and took one look at me and asked if I needed a doctor. This shocked me a little. I must have looked bad. It was the mud on my work clothes – they probably thought I'd lost my memory and was wondering the countryside aimlessly.

"No! No! I'm fine thanks – just had an argument with a stream – shouldn't have crossed it in my good clothes. Silly of me. Must look a mess."

"Well, perhaps a bit muddy," one of them laughed before they all disappeared into the nearby wood.

A man suddenly came running round the corner. "Thought I saw a leopard," he said breathlessly as he passed by."Did the others go this way?"

"They're not far ahead," I said.

"Nice golden Lab," he shouted over his shoulder, "mine's black."

Archie isn't a golden Labrador – he just masquerades as one, but he does have a good nose – and by this time he had his nose to the ground and was running after the man into the wood.

"But he said he saw a leopard this way!" I called after Archie, "I'm going this way!" and I went in the opposite direction to Archie.

Archie has a highly developed sense of his own importance but the one thing he hates is being ignored and he loves biscuits, so he was soon by my side again.

"Find the leopard! Find the leopard!" I shouted.

He immediately turned and went back into the wood. This time I decided to follow him. Maybe, the man had imagined he'd seen a leopard. It happens.

Or, maybe, he really had seen my leopard and my leopard had followed the man without me noticing – leopards are good at lurking.

It was dense woodland and a leopard could easily hide up a tree and leap down on a passer-by and kill them in an instant. This was a tricky situation. There was a group of walkers who couldn't be that far ahead and then the lone man, then Archie and then me. My leopard would be spoilt for choice but would probably choose the man because he could pick him off easily before anyone noticed. In fact, he was probably dragging him up a tree at this very moment. The question of my culpability arose again – it would be entirely my fault. When the man shouted, 'I thought I saw a leopard!' I should have shouted back, 'You did! You did! Beware! He'll eat you!', something like that, but what did I do? Nothing!

Why? Because he's my leopard and he's my secret and I don't want to share him. But I hope he doesn't eat the man – he seemed nice.

I heard a twig snap behind me and swung round ready to face my leopard. There was a rustle in the nearby tree. I looked up and saw beautiful spots high up in the shadows. My leopard.

"Quick this way, Archie," I called out and for once Archie did as he was told.

We walked slowly out of the wood and I knew my leopard was following us. We'd have to take the long route home skirting the villages so that he wouldn't be seen. I kept walking and didn't look back. Neither did Archie. We didn't want to look my leopard in the eye and give him the impression that we'd noticed him.

At last we got home. I filled the bucket with cat food and filled the fish pond with water and waited on the other side of the gate with Archie. After a short while, me and Archie heard the crunching of cat food. Now we knew for certain my leopard had followed us home, we went into the house. We were exhausted. It had all been very emotionally draining. That night I slept well and so did Archie and we both got up late and we were still exhausted. The first thing I did was drag myself outside to check on my leopard. He was obviously exhausted too because he was lying on his back and I saw then that *he* was a *he,* which meant that my intuition had been right. He was snoring loudly and the sun was out, so I guessed he'd sleep most of the day and not go on any more escapades.

When I eventually got to work, it was practically lunch time, and everyone went quiet, when I walked in, and Daisy, who's after my job, said, "The boss was looking for you – wants to see you in his office as soon as you come in." She smiled sweetly. She's one of those duplicitous people who smile sweetly before they slit your throat.

Usually this sort of thing makes me feel very bad and I have to buy myself a bar of chocolate to make life worth living, but now I had a leopard living in my garden, it didn't worry me one bit. In fact, I felt sorry for her because of her limited perspective and lack of leopard awareness and was able to say with absolute sincerity, "That's good. Maybe he's going to sack me and give you my job. That'll make you happy."

Daisy's face fell and she stuttered, "Well maybe...well yes...", and her face went red. Several people in the office actually laughed out loud when I strolled past her and straight into my boss's office without knocking.

"You've not been yourself recently," my boss said, as soon as I sat down. "Your work has been suffering."

Since my work involved persuading people to buy things they didn't actually need, I now knew this was a good thing.

"I know," I said with a smile.

There was silence.

He cleared his throat, "Lily, we've really, really, valued your contribution," he hesitated. "Have you considered the twenty thousand...made up your mind yet? I need an answer or..."

He droned on about procedures, and verbal warnings, and written warnings, and tribunals and, of course, he didn't want to go down that route, but he would, if necessary. He must have noticed the glazed expression on my face because he suddenly asked, "Are you listening?"

"I think I'll go now." I stood up quickly and almost ran out of the room and out of the building before he could catch me. If he couldn't catch me, he couldn't sack me and I might need the job, if my leopard awareness thing didn't work out.

It was still sunny and warm when I got home. I checked on my leopard and he was asleep on his back, with his legs sticking straight up, so I took a chance and let Archie out into the back garden. Archie was pleased to be out and had the sense not to go anywhere near my leopard. Recklessly, we both fell asleep in the sun. Archie was on the grass and I was in the hammock.

Archie woke me up with his barking. I fell out of the hammock just in time to see my leopard leap to his feet and hide crouching in the grass. There was somebody at my front door. I crept round the side of my house to see who it was. My boss! Come to sack me? It was imperative he didn't get the chance to sack me on the spot, so I told Archie to be quiet and we ran out of the back garden and down the lane.

It was a lovely day so we just kept on walking. We must have been walking for about an hour when Archie disappeared into the brambles at the side of the lane and came out carrying a banana. He looked at me sheepishly. Obviously, he wanted the banana all to himself but I made him hand it over.

I took a good look at it. Normally I don't eat bananas people have thrown away under hedges but on inspection this banana was a perfectly good banana which shouldn't have been thrown away in the first place. So I peeled it there and then and we ate it between us. The banana gave us more energy and we walked on at a faster pace. I say *we walked* – Archie doesn't walk in a straight line if he can help it. Most of the time he's loitering and sniffing, lingering at corners and going round in circles and even retracing his steps, and when he's feeling particularly carefree, he bursts into high speed running.

We were happy. The only thing that was missing was our leopard – I say *our* because I'd decided to share my leopard with someone and Archie was the obvious candidate. But was our leopard missing? I glanced sideways and there, peering out from under the hawthorn hedge, were a pair of familiar gleaming eyes, "Hello there! You followed us. You clever leopard," I greeted him warmly. "Should have known you would. Found any rabbits yet?"

Lots of rabbits live along this lane and they would make tasty snacks for our leopard, which is a great shame for the rabbits, but a leopard has to eat and dried cat food probably has rabbits in it anyway, I now realised.

Even Archie seemed pleased to see our leopard and we'd both begun to trust him a little bit and thought that he might not try to eat us, as long as there were plenty of rabbits about.

Leopards are big but they are also very good at camouflage and creeping about unseen, so it wasn't as difficult as I first imagined to travel with a leopard practically at my heels.

The thing about travelling is that, once you've started, it's very hard to stop. I suppose that's why early man crossed over from Africa into Europe and from Europe into North America and on into Asia, or was it the other way round? My point is – once started, there's no stopping in the travelling.

That night, me and Archie slept under a hedge. I say *slept*. We discovered that leopards don't sleep at night at all, instead they go out hunting. We could hear him pacing about and every now and then we heard squealing sounds as he ate another rabbit. We felt sorry for the rabbits but, as long as he was eating them, he wasn't eating us and he kept at a safe distance – Archie had one eye open just in case.

By morning, we were tired and shivering and our leopard was now fast asleep under the hedge. We could hear him snoring contentedly. He'd eaten a lot of rabbits and would probably sleep all day. Me and Archie had only eaten one banana between us and were very hungry and so we set off in search of food. We headed for the supermarket, which I reckoned was only about three miles away, if we went across the fields. I knew supermarkets threw away food willy-nilly so we had a good chance of easy pickings from the bins, if we got there before opening time.

The dew was on the grass and it soaked my sandals and soon my feet were sore and, added to all that, I started worrying about our leopard. What if he woke up and found we weren't there and followed someone else – a small child on a bicycle or an old man with a stick – they'd be easy targets. We had to find food soon and get back to him. We started running and when we got to the supermarket, we dashed round to where the bins were.

Some of the bins were locked but most weren't. I found one full of packets of food and rummaged through and discovered some day old muffins and out of date orange juice for me and some chicken legs for Archie. In another bin, there were trainers with marks on them. I chose some pink ones and took off my wet sandals and threw them in the bin and put on the pink trainers.

16

We heard a car approaching. We quickly ducked down and hid behind the bins and, in the same moment, we saw a flash of spots leap high and disappear into the food bin. Our leopard had followed us after all – even though I'm pretty sure leopards are supposed to sleep all day! It's not every day that a supermarket has a leopard in one of its bins and I knew that, if he was discovered, that would be it. He'd be splashed all over the news and our lives would be ruined. The three of us would become national legends and, if he ate anyone, we'd become national villains.

The car stopped near the bins and a young man got out and was walking towards the bin with our leopard in it. Up until now, our leopard had been noisily searching the bin and we'd heard the crunching of bones which probably meant he'd found another pack of chicken legs. Now he was quiet. We watched helplessly as the young man approached the bin and our leopard's head popped up with some chicken legs dangling from his mouth and his greenish-golden eyes staring intently at the young man. Fortunately, the young man didn't expect to see a leopard so early in the morning, and so he walked on without noticing and went into the supermarket through the back door.

"Phew! That was close," I said to Archie, "I think it's time we left."

We ran back the way we'd come and found a quiet spot by a stream where Archie ate the chicken legs and I ate two muffins and drank half the orange juice. Our leopard lay down nearby and we pretended we hadn't seen him and soon he was purring loudly, which pleased us no end and hopefully meant he was beginning to accept us as friends rather than a tasty meal.

Archie stretched out on the grassy bank and I lay on my back and looked up at the sky. It was mostly blue with the occasional fluffy cloud floating lazily by. This is the life, I thought, as the sounds of the purring leopard relaxed me so much I fell asleep. Going to sleep was a big mistake, I decided, when I woke up and found the leopard standing over me and he wasn't purring and where was Archie?

You can't afford to let your guard down when there's a leopard on the loose and I'd done just that. My life flashed before my eyes – I was already thirty; I was childless; I worked in a worthless job; I was on the run from my boss. But then my thoughts turned more positive – my mother loved me; Archie loved me; I'd found a leopard in my garden; I'd been brave; I'd been resourceful – at this point, our leopard opened his mouth and yawned and I saw teeth as sharp as knives, just before he licked me gently on the face. I say *gently* but it was a painful, rasping sensation but I could tell he meant to be gentle by the look in his greenish-golden eyes. I kept perfectly still and heard Archie barking in the distance and our leopard heard him too. He lifted his head to listen before he turned and leapt away.

Archie rushed up to me and looked over his shoulder. I followed his gaze and saw a line of people spread out across a field in the distance and heading our way. Maybe they were looking for something. Maybe somebody had disappeared and they were searching for clues. And that somebody could be me! Should I give myself up? It was the wisest thing to do, but, first and foremost, I had to make sure our leopard wasn't discovered.

I tidied myself up as best I could – running my fingers threw my hair and dusting the mud off my clothes – and made straight for the line of people. Archie followed me reluctantly. As I got nearer, I saw that some of the people were policemen. I began to rehearse what I was going to say, like – *I'm out walking with my dog* or *I'm undertaking a natural history research project* or *I got disorientated and ended up here. I think I need to see a doctor.*

Instead, I just said, "Hello. Looking for something?"

"Surprised you haven't heard." The policeman looked at me suspiciously as he stroked Archie, "There's been an armed robbery. Pictures stolen."

I sighed with relief. They weren't after me and our leopard. "Anybody hurt?" I asked.

"No. What are you doing here?"

"Live nearby," I lied. "Taking my dog for a walk."

He got out his notebook, "Just for the record, what's your name and address?"

"Mary Smith," I lied again, "6 Main Street...the village over there". I pointed to the village in the distance.

He must have known the name of it because he didn't ask me any more questions and said, "Enjoy your walk", and caught up with the others who were already crossing the next field.

Archie and I walked on nonchalantly without looking back and I began to realise that perhaps it wasn't the cleverest thing to have lied about my name and address. If the policeman had a phone in his pocket and

19

he checked up on the details, I'd be exposed as a liar and most likely accused of taking part in the armed robbery. But there were more important things to worry about – like would they come across our leopard in their search and, if they did, would he try to eat them?

It was at that moment that I heard a sound behind me. I turned and there was our leopard, creeping up on me and preparing to pounce. I stood tall – people in Africa do this when they come across lions and want to steal the lions' kill – standing tall definitely worked for those people – the lions turned and ran – I saw it on the telly. Our leopard hasn't seen the telly and kept on creeping up on me and pounced and knocked me off my feet and licked me right on the face, and then leapt away looking very pleased with himself.

I stood up feeling slighted. I know he hadn't eaten me but he *had* knocked me down. Then I saw the funny side and started laughing. Leopards can teach you quite a lot about life – like it's not as serious as you think and you never have things in control and... Our leopard reappeared dragging something through the grass. I hoped it wasn't a dead body.

He dragged it right up to me and left it at my feet. It was a large painting with big holes in it where his teeth had been.

"Thanks," I said and took a chance and patted him and he looked up at me with his greenish-golden eyes. He really is a beautiful leopard and I'm getting very fond of him, even if he'll eat me one day.

I picked up the painting and took a good look at it, while Archie sat beside me and waited and our leopard flopped down and went to sleep. The painting wasn't bad, as far as paintings go – the sort of painting I like, full of bright colours and tropical trees, like Gauguin painted.

I began to wonder if, in fact, this was a Gauguin and those armed robbers had stolen it from the Stately Home nearby and panicked and dropped it and, it just so happened, our leopard was passing by at the time and he picked it up and brought it to me, his friend. It was feasible. Cats bring you mice – our leopard brings me paintings worth millions. It was an exciting prospect and it made my heart race. Now, I had a beautiful leopard with greenish-golden eyes *and* a Gauguin. I was the luckiest person in the world.

"Our lives are full of beauty," I said to Archie, poetically. He wagged his tail. He could tell I was happy. A second later it started to rain, which is often the way when you say things are going well. It's called tempting fate.

"Should be safe to go home now," I said, tucking the painting under my arm and looking down at Archie who was sopping wet. I heard splashing and saw our leopard leaping about in the stream. Evidently, leopards like water but I don't think he's that keen on heavy rain because he was soon sloping along close to the ground and looking pretty miserable.

I hadn't realised we'd walked so far and it was almost dark when we got home. We approached the house cautiously down the lane and in through the back garden gate. I opened the door of the garden shed so that our leopard could shelter from the rain but his ears went flat in disgust and I thought he was going to whack me one with his paw but instead he squeezed under the shed and all you could see was his tail sticking out.

"Suit yourself," I said.

Archie and I went into the house and I placed the Gauguin carefully against the kitchen wall – it was dripping wet and the colours looked even brighter. There was a pile of letters on the front door mat and I could tell at a glance that most of them were rubbish, or bills, which amounts to the same thing. There was one addressed by hand and I recognised it immediately. It was from my boss. I opened it quickly to get it over and done with. Since becoming leopard aware, I've realised that it's best to face up to things or else you get in even deeper.

The letter was deceptively friendly, all about how he was sorry he didn't have longer to talk to me at work, and sorry he'd missed me today but he'd like to meet me tomorrow, somewhere of my own choosing. Tomorrow was today, so I'd missed the meeting, thank goodness, and there was nothing else to do but go to bed.

I looked at myself in the mirror. I was covered in dirt from head to foot and my hair stuck out at all angles like a mad woman and my teeth had bits of muffin stuck to them. It was definitely time for a clean-up. I looked down at Archie – dogs are self cleaning and already the dirt had dropped off him and onto my carpet.

I had a shower and went to bed and decided, if we went travelling tomorrow, I'd wear proper clothes and take my credit card with me – because living off rejected supermarket food might not be sustainable, especially if you travelled to a country without supermarkets.

The next morning, I woke with a start and a sense that something was wrong. I looked out of my back window and there was our leopard asleep in the grass. I wondered if he'd been out hunting all night and, if he had, I hoped it was rabbits. I checked on Archie. He was asleep in his basket. I checked on the painting. It was still there leaning against the kitchen wall. So far so good. I went to the front of the house. There was a police car parked outside and a commotion going on. A policeman was standing between a woman and a man who were yelling at each other. I ducked down under the window sill and quietly opened the window so I could hear what they were saying.

"It was definitely his dog. It's always in my garden and, this time, it's gone too far. He's eaten them! *All* my chickens!" The woman began to cry.

"My dog was in all night!"

"Can you prove that, sir?" the policeman asked.

"Yes, the door was locked!"

"That's no proof," the woman sobbed.

"Ok. Ok. We'll get to the bottom of this." I took a quick look – the policeman had his notebook out.

I crawled away from the window knowing it was our leopard who was to blame – he'd been out on a hunt and come across some chickens and it was just a matter of luck the woman hadn't been eaten as well!

It was time to leave for good before our leopard was discovered. My phone started ringing – it was from my boss so I switched it off – we had to make a quick getaway. I threw on jeans, a t-shirt and the pink trainers, grabbed my car keys, my credit card and my phone and was out of the front door with Archie at my heels.

"Good morning," I said to the policeman and the man and woman who were still arguing right next to my car. They moved aside so that me and Archie could get in. My hands were shaking as I started up the engine and drove up the main street and down the back lane.

"Stay!" I told Archie.

I rushed through the back garden and into the kitchen and grabbed the Gauguin and ran back to the car. Our leopard woke up, stretched out his beautiful spotted body and silently followed me to the car.

"You'll have to sit in the back seat," I told him opening the back door.

He snarled at me.

I opened the passenger door where Archie was sitting on the front seat. Archie barked and our leopard snarled but, surprisingly, Archie won and our leopard turned away and jumped onto the back seat. He curled up and started to doze off – he was obviously stuffed full of chickens. Even though he was curled up, you could still see his spots above the car window – he's a big leopard.

I put the Gauguin in the boot and drove off. I'd never driven with a leopard in my car before and it wasn't so bad for the first fifty miles – even when we passed through cities and got stuck in traffic jams and people glanced sideways from their cars or looked down on us from buses and saw our leopard sleeping on the back seat – even then they just smiled, probably thinking he was an extra large stuffed toy. I wouldn't be surprised if they said to the person next to them on the bus, *That's realistic, bet it cost a bomb.*

At one point, I think our leopard must have yawned or scratched his ear or something like that because, when we stopped at some traffic lights, a young boy, sitting in the back seat of a Four by Four, started pointing and shouting and jumping up and down. His mother began telling him off – you could tell by the twisted expression on her face. I just smiled sweetly and was glad when the lights changed and I drove off before them. Most drivers of Four by Fours have never had a leopard or anything like it in their car. I bet they'd like to have one. Or maybe not because having a leopard in your car does have its down sides – especially when he wakes up after fifty miles.

I knew our leopard was awake when he patted me across the back of my head. I say *patted* because his claws weren't out, but it was more like a clout and I swerved the car into the oncoming traffic and yelled. Yelling wasn't a good idea – it frightened our leopard and he started clawing at the back seat – this is where he finally eats me, I thought.

I turned down a lane, stopped the car, jumped out and opened the back door. Our leopard leapt out immediately and went and did a long pee in the grass. I suppose I should be grateful he didn't pee in the car. As soon as he'd peed, he jumped straight back into the car and went to sleep again – when you've been out all night hunting, you definitely need a good day's sleep.

Me and Archie sat on the roadside to calm down – having a semi-domesticated leopard in your car is a stressful business.

I'd travelled fifty miles and was heading for Scotland. It was the wildest place I knew and I hoped they'd be plenty of deer there for our leopard to eat. Me and Archie jumped back into the car and I drove off at speed because we had to get as far as we could while our leopard was asleep.

At last we passed a sign saying *Scotland Welcomes You* and then it began to rain. I had to find a place that was leopard friendly – deer for eating, water for swimming in, sun for sleeping in during the day. Scotland had the deer and the water but it was beginning to look as though the sun would be missing.

I turned left and headed for the coast and drove for miles and miles until it got dark. We'd just passed a pub called the *Laughing Horse*, which was an unusual name for a pub but quite catchy, when our leopard yawned loudly. I looked in my mirror. A pair of greenish-golden eyes stared back at me. Time to stop before our leopard decided to give me another whack on the back of the head. I drove along until I came to an area of woodland with a parking place and picnic tables. There was no one about so I parked the car and let our leopard out. He slunk out slowly, looked around and suddenly put on an amazing spurt of speed and shimmied straight up a nearby oak tree and let his legs drape casually down on either side of the branch. He looked down at us cheekily – he was showing off. Me and Archie pretended not to be impressed. I didn't think our leopard was going out night hunting because he seemed to be settling down for a snooze up there. He must've eaten a lot of chickens and I think leopards only have to eat once every three days, anyway.

"Come on Archie. Let's get something to eat," I said as we set off for the pub, together.

We walked for about a mile back to the *Laughing Horse*. I poked my head through the door and saw three men sitting at the bar and a young man with blonde hair behind the bar.

"Are dogs allowed?"

The three men nodded, unsmiling. It's probably my English accent putting them off – good job they don't know I've got a semi-domesticated leopard snoozing up a tree only a mile away.

"Dogs are welcome," the young blonde man smiled at me and Archie.

We went in and I ordered fish and chips and a beer for me and a beef sandwich for Archie and we sat down in a corner. The three men carried on drinking and Archie didn't go up to them and make friends – which was a sure sign they were not the sort of people to give biscuits to dogs. Archie doesn't care what people look like or even if they smell bad, but he's a good judge of character. I envy him that.

I don't have Archie's moral depth when it comes to looks. I care what people look like and what they smell like, for that matter. The three men did not look appealing – there was a middle-aged man with grey hair, an older man with a bald head and a younger one with a leery red face and black hair and they were dressed in various shades of grey.

"Come far?" the middle aged man with the grey hair turned and called out to me.

"From Norfolk," I lied.

"Norfolk. I used to live there. Which part?"

"Oh, I don't live there. That's where I started out from... yesterday," I lied again. It's called thinking on your feet.

"So where do you come from...originally?"

"Uh...Africa." At least five hundred years ago, I muttered to myself.

"That explains it." The older man with a bald head gave me an insincere smile and I saw that he had no teeth. The younger red faced man leered at me. I bet he's got teeth missing too. I've got a thing about teeth.

At this point, the young blonde man brought my fish and chips and Archie's beef sandwich, which was a relief. That conversation was getting trickier by the minute.

The fish was dry and the chips tasted like cardboard but I ate them hungrily and Archie ate his beef sandwich in fifteen seconds flat. At least the beer was tasty.

"I'll get your dog some water," the young blonde man called out from behind the bar. He disappeared into the back of the pub and brought a bowl of water right over to Archie and placed it in front of him.

"Where you staying?" he asked – he had a full set of teeth.

"Oh...well...nowhere," I said.

"Nowhere?"

Here we go again – "I'm camping," I lied.

"You'd better watch out," shouted the red faced one, "There's a big man-eating cat about!" He laughed at the ridiculous idea and the other two joined in.

My heart started to race. Our leopard had been spotted! The game was up!

"A big cat?" My voice squeaked out.

"Where've you been? It's all over the news. They reckon a big cat ate a load of chickens down south." The red-faced one gave me a leery smile.

"Probably a fox," I said.

"Neighbour swore it was a big cat," the red-faced one added.

"People'll say anything to be on the news," the old bald man gave me an unfriendly stare.

They went on talking amongst themselves about big cat sightings. I'd stopped listening and was busy worrying about our leopard dozing in the oak tree, when I heard the word *Gauguin*.

"Gauguin?" I piped up.

"Where *have* you been?" the old bald man said irritably. He was the sort of person who would shoot our leopard and mount his head over a mantelpiece.

"Never mind him," the young blonde man muttered as he picked up my empty plate. "He's a narrow minded bigot."

"You don't say," I laughed. "Gauguin, what's that all about?"

"Robbers stole a whole bunch of paintings down in England."

My mouth dropped open and I must have looked pretty astonished because he said, "You seem surprised."

"Oh...not really. Have they caught them yet... got any of the paintings back?"

"Nope. Probably out of the country by now." He cleared away my empty beer glass. "'Fraid we're closing. See you tomorrow, maybe?" he said, as I got up to go.

"Maybe," I said.

The three men at the bar had already left. I went outside pushing past the men who were standing smoking cigarettes in the doorway.

"Goodnight," leered the red-faced one. "Watch out for big cats."

"I will," I shouted over my shoulder as I saw the shadowy shape of our leopard walk right past me and across the pub car park.

"Did you see that!" yelled the red-faced one.

"Quick inside!" The grey haired one shouted, "Watch out!"

"Think you've all had a bit too much to drink," I shouted back.

I strode away in the same direction as our leopard and heard the old bald man shout after me, "Bloody foreigner!"

I looked behind me. They'd gone back into the pub for safety. It was at this point that murderous thoughts leapt into my mind. I could set our leopard on them and who would be bloody then! The feeling soon went away – it wouldn't be fair on our leopard – he preferred eating rabbits and chickens.

What if the three men told the police they'd seen a big cat crossing the pub car park right there in front of them? Chances are the police would think they were drunk, as usual. They were probably well known around here – in the pub every night propping up the bar and terrorising tourists.

But it was all getting more worrying by the minute. More and more people suspected that a big cat was roaming wild and some people had seen it and others would be saying they'd definitely seen it, even though they hadn't – because everyone was searching for something special in their lives. People never think about what it's really like to look after a leopard – all the trouble they can cause you and how they whack you over the head, if you don't let them out of your car after a long journey.

And then there was the question of the art theft and the painting in my car. Was it really a stolen Gauguin? And, if it was – and I was stopped by the police and they looked in the car and saw our leopard on the back seat and then looked in the boot and found the Gauguin in there – I'd be arrested on the spot and charged with unlawful ownership of a dangerous animal AND with possession of stolen property. They'd never believe our leopard just turned up and, later on, one afternoon, gave me a masterpiece by Gauguin.

I needed to think long and hard about what to do next. I didn't get the chance. I heard quick footsteps behind me.

"Wait! Hold on a minute!" It was the young blond-haired man from the pub, "Did you see it?" He was out of breath.

"See what?" I replied innocently.

"The big cat, of course," he said.

"No. They've had too much to drink," I said with conviction.

"You're probably right but they sounded certain. They were really scared."

"Serves them right."

"That's harsh. You'd be scared if you'd just seen a big cat," he said.

"If I saw a leopard in the grass, I'd think it was wonderful."

"It wasn't in any grass. It was lurking about in the dark outside the pub," he hesitated, "You said leopard. Why leopard?"

Damn, I've got to be more careful, "I like leopards that's all."

"You an expert on leopards?" he asked.

He was getting far too friendly and we were getting nearer and nearer the car and I thought I could hear our leopard behind us and Archie thought so too because he kept stopping and looking nervously over his shoulder. "Hadn't you better be getting back to the pub?" I said.

"Expect I should. See you again. I hope." He turned and disappeared into the darkness. I heard him shout over his shoulder, "Leopard in the grass!?"

He was pretty crazy but I liked him and, if it hadn't been for our leopard creeping about in the dark, I could have got to know him a lot better but, if it hadn't been for our leopard, I'd never have met him in the first place. It's called one thing leading to another.

I checked to see if the Gauguin was still in the boot of the car – it was and was looking good, even though it had been through a lot.

That night, me and Archie slept in the car and our leopard kept a lookout high up in the tree. We woke at first light and our leopard came down from the tree and paced around the car until I let him into the back seat. Our leopard now thinks that the back seat is his den. I bet he would eat the first person who tried to get in there before him. Me and Archie pretended that we never wanted to go anywhere near it in the first place. It's called knowing when you're beaten.

I drove off in search of a more isolated spot where our leopard could live in peace. I drove past the Laughing Horse, past a couple of cottages and a school and turned right, down a narrow winding lane. You could tell hardly anybody went this way because there was grass growing in the middle. Eventually, we came to a forest. This was a great place for our leopard to hunt and he'd be getting hungry soon. He hadn't eaten since the great chicken fest and, when you're sharing a car with a leopard, it isn't wise to let him go hungry.

I drove the car right into the forest and parked it off the lane between the trees. I got out and checked to see if it could be spotted from the lane. It couldn't. So far so good. We could stay here while I decided what to do next. I let Archie and our leopard out of the car and straight away our leopard ran off through the trees. He was probably looking for a tree with a comfortable branch so he could sleep the day away before going out on a night hunt. Archie ran after him, probably because he's a nosey dog and likes to know what our leopard's up to. I didn't think they'd go far because our leopard would be very sleepy after being on the lookout all night.

I found a quiet sunny glade and sat down with my back against a tree. I decided that I would decide what to do next, later. This was a mistake – if you don't act while you've got the chance, you've only got yourself to blame.

A gunshot rang out and I jumped up in terror. Someone was shooting at our leopard! Archie came running through the trees towards me, behind him, a man with a shot gun, behind him, our leopard in stalking mode. I had to choose between the man with a gun and our leopard. I didn't want to choose. The best I could do was give them both a fighting chance.

"Watch out there's a leopard behind you! Watch out! Watch out! Watch out!" I flung my arms about and screeched and jumped up and down like a mad woman.

The man stopped dead in his tracks, our leopard leapt up the nearest tree and Archie ran to my side. The man lowered his shot gun and approached me and Archie cautiously. Archie was growling and baring his teeth – he can look pretty fierce when he wants to.

"Calm down!" the man said, condescendingly. Guns give people a false sense of their own importance and our leopard thought so too because he leapt out of the tree and knocked the man right off his feet. The man's head hit a stone. He lay there motionless with our leopard standing astride him and growling. I think our leopard would definitely have eaten him if I hadn't rushed up and grabbed our leopard's tail and shouted "NO! NO! NO!" I was being stupidly brave but I guess our leopard was almost totally domesticated by this time because he just slunk away with a sideways snarl and disappeared into the forest.

"Wake up! Wake up!" I slapped the man across the face in a panic. He groaned. There was blood on the ground. There was nothing for it but to get him into the car and drive him to the nearest hospital as fast as possible.

"Can you stand up?" I shouted. He opened his eyes and looked at me, reproachfully.

"I've got to get you to a hospital." I tried to pull him towards the car but he was too heavy, "You've been eating too many takeaways," I said.

He shook his head. "I'll crawl," he groaned feebly. He pushed himself to a sitting position and crawled to the car. "A leopard," he gasped as he collapsed into the back seat.

"It smells bad in here," he complained as I slammed the door shut. Our leopard had returned and he wasn't at all pleased that there was a man in his den. He rushed up to the car, leapt on top of it and roamed about in a mood and then he started roaring loudly. We'd never heard him roar before – it sounded like someone sawing wood.

"No time for that!" I shouted at our leopard angrily, "You brought it on yourself. We're off to the hospital. Quick! In you get Archie," I held open the front door for Archie.

I started up the engine and our leopard stayed on top of the car as I drove slowly out of the trees and on to the lane. I looked in my rear view mirror. The man was slumped in the back, his eyes closed. I hoped he didn't realise there was a leopard on top of the car.

"Leopard on top of the car," I heard him mutter.

"Damn!" I said out loud and drove on faster. Our leopard jumped off the car and I glimpsed his beautiful spotted form, as he disappeared in a flash into the forest. I was worried. Would we ever see him again?

I drove at high speed down lanes until I came to a town, screeched to a halt in front of a Health Centre and dashed inside.

"Badly injured man in the car!" I gasped.

"I'll call an ambulance," the receptionist said. "We only do basic First Aid here. Nurse!" she shouted.

A nurse appeared and ran outside to the car with me. I opened the back door.

"What's that smell?" she held her nose.

"It's not me!" the man muttered.

"Well, you're talking. That's a good sign," the nurse said.

"Attacked by a leopard," he moaned.

"That's not such a good sign," the nurse said as she took a quick look at the man's head. "That's a nasty cut you've got. Keep still. Wait there." She ran back into the Health Centre.

"I'm not planning on going anywhere," the man muttered, sarcastically.

The nurse came rushing back with a wheelchair and together we managed to get him into it. The nurse wheeled him off into the Health Centre.

"Stay there," I said to Archie, who was all for following the nurse, to check out the biscuit situation in the Health Centre.

I sat in the Waiting Room and after about ten minutes the nurse came out of a Treatment room and took me to one side.

"Will he be ok?" I asked.

"Yes, I think so. I've cleaned up the cut and checked him over. We're waiting for the ambulance. Are you a relative?"

"No I was out...walking my dog...in the forest and he came along with a gun..."

"With a gun?" She looked worried.

"Only shooting rabbits or deer, I expect."

"And then what happened?"

"Well he just... sort of...fell over and banged his head," I said.

"He keeps going on about a leopard. Said it leapt right out at him."

"I know. I know. Weird isn't it...must be the bump on the head..." I hesitated.

The nurse was giving me a searching look, which was a sure sign that she was getting suspicious of the whole story.

"I expect he wants to get in on the act. People'll do anything to be famous, nowadays," she said.

"In on the act?"

"Heard it on the news earlier. Story of a big cat jumping out and attacking people at a pub not that far from here. They're sending out search parties. You were there when he fell? You definitely didn't see a leopard lurking about, did you?" she smiled.

"Definitely not. I think I would have noticed. Don't you?" I laughed. I'm getting very good at lying. "I'll be off now," I said. "Glad he's going to be ok."

I left the Health Centre in a hurry, jumped in my car and we were off back towards the forest. I tried to remain calm but it was obvious things were really getting out of control. I looked down at Archie – he looked glum and was shivering. He always knows when I'm in a state. Our leopard wasn't our leopard any more. Our secret was out. He'd made the National news and people had already started making things up – saying he'd attacked the men in the pub, which he hadn't – but now he really had attacked a man and that would soon get out and, if they saw our leopard, they'd shoot him on

37

the spot. I put my foot on the break and pulled over to the side of the road and sat looking straight ahead. It's time, I thought. It's time to give him up. I can't keep him to myself any longer. I'll have to tell the truth. I looked down at Archie, he whimpered.

"He's not our leopard any more – if we don't tell them, they'll shoot him. It's for the best," then I started sobbing loudly. Archie curled up into a ball and whimpered again.

I wiped my face dry, turned the car around and drove to the local police station.

"Wait there," I said to Archie.

I walked straight into the police station and up to the desk.

"Morning," an overweight policeman said, looking me up and down. "What happened to you?"

"It's the big cat. I know where he is," I said.

The policeman's eyes widened, "Do you really", he sighed. "Strangely enough, you're not the first person today." There was a distinctively sarcastic tone in his voice, "Tell me *your* story, then."

I was emotionally distraught, "It's not a **story!** He's in the forest waiting for me. He'll come quietly. There's no need to shoot him. I'll get him to you in the back of my car. He likes it in there."

The policeman shook his head, "Look miss, you're wasting my time."

"I've got proof. Follow me," I said.

The policeman called out to someone in another room, "Watch the desk for a minute," and followed me out to the car.

I opened the car door, "Smell that," I shouted. "That's what a leopard smells like!"

The policeman drew back in disgust, "Look miss, you need to get your car cleaned and you need to see someone. Follow me."

I didn't follow him. I stood on the pavement and stared after him before getting into my car and driving off slowly.

You couldn't really blame the policeman – it's called, truth being stranger than fiction. But he definitely lacked leopard awareness. What now? The policeman didn't believe me, but, maybe, the media would and they could organise a *Bring the Leopard Back Alive* campaign.

I cheered up – mostly because I hadn't been believed and so our leopard was still *our* leopard in a small way. But once I told the media that would definitely be the end. He'd be breaking news and the world's property. But I suppose that's better than being shot.

I turned the car around again and drove back into town and eventually spotted a grimy sign saying *The Gazette*. The sign hung above a shabby shop front. It looked as though they'd been hit by the recession and needed a good story.

"Back in a minute," I said to Archie. He looked up at me with a resigned expression – he doesn't trust my timekeeping.

The door creaked as I opened it and it took a while for my eyes to adjust to the gloom. A man of about my age, with a haunted look and a cigarette in his mouth, glanced at me with his eyes narrowed as though he was taking part in a gangster movie. I half expected him to draw a gun. When he spoke he sounded surprisingly meek, "Got some good news for me?"

"A scoop," I said.

"That'll be the day," he laughed, sitting down on a worn out sofa. "Take a seat. Tell me more."

"It's about the big cat," I sat down on the other worn out sofa. "We've got to save him before they hunt him down. It's urgent!"

He sighed, "Everybody's got a big cat story this morning."

"Mine's unique," I said. "It's true."

"OK. Start from the beginning. Name's Gordon by the way."

I didn't tell him my name. "It's a long story. Can I bring my dog in? He's waiting in the car."

"Be my guest. I like dogs," he said.

I went and got Archie out of the car. After being coped up in the car all morning, he was very pleased to be out and he liked Gordon immediately, mostly because Gordon made us a cup of tea and there were biscuits. I sat down and sipped the tea and Archie ate biscuits.

"What's your story then?"

"Aren't you going to take notes?" I said.

"Got a good memory," he said.

"Well," I began, "it all started about two weeks ago when I woke up one morning, looked out of my window and saw him."

"Him?"

"Our leopard..."

"So the big cat is a leopard?"

"Yes and he was hiding in the long grass in my back garden. I didn't know he was a he at the time...I only got a glimpse, greenish-golden eyes and a beautiful shimmering spotted body..."

Gordon got up and went over to a desk where an old computer stood, "Go on. Don't mind me." He sat down at the desk and started to type.

"Well," I continued, "I didn't call the police or anybody, for that matter. I wanted to keep our leopard a secret. It was so wonderful having a leopard in my back garden, I didn't want to spoil it. Can you understand that?"

"Sort of," Gordon was looking very puzzled. "Why d'you say *our* leopard. Are you married? Did your husband see it too?"

"No, I'm not married," I replied, somewhat tetchily. "Me and Archie, he belongs to me and Archie."

Gordon was typing very fast now.

"So I kept our leopard for a whole week in my back garden," I told him.

Gordon's eyes were wide with scepticism, "You kept a real live leopard for a whole week in your back garden, just like that?"

Already, I could tell it wasn't going well. Perhaps I should have stopped talking at that point and just walked straight out of there. But I didn't. "Well, there were a few incidents. We sort of went camping one night and he ate quite a lot of rabbits and later on he hid in a supermarket bin and after that he found a Gauguin and brought it to me as a present and then he ate a whole load of chickens, and he thought the back seat of my car was his den, and so he..."

41

"Hold it," Gordon stopped typing. "Did you say Gauguin? You can't expect me to believe that. It's, well, unlikely...to say the least."

"But it's true. I'll show you the Gauguin, if you like. Wait there." I rushed out to the car, got the Gauguin out of the boot and ran back in. Archie was sitting beside Gordon and eating another biscuit.

"There!" I leaned the Gauguin against the desk with a flourish. "And that's where our leopard carried it. See the holes. His teeth made those holes."

I could see Gordon was impressed and for a moment I thought he was going to believe me but then he looked up and smiled, "It's a good story. I'll give you that and I'll write it up...might sell a few copies, you never know. Did you paint it yourself? It's not bad."

I just stood there with my mouth open. Gordon patted Archie on the head, "I bet it was you, Archie, wasn't it? You bit it and made these holes." Archie wagged his tail. He now adores Gordon because of the biscuits.

It dawned on me that Gordon wasn't going to believe me, no matter what. I should have made up an everyday story – like me spotting something in the forest, which could have been a leopard but probably wasn't but was worth investigating anyway. Then, he might have believed me – because some people would rather believe something ordinary and uninspiring – it comforts them and puts them in a better light, by comparison. It's called the comfort of everyday monotony.

"So are you going to help me organise a *Bring the Leopard Back Alive* campaign or not!?" I glared at him.

"I'll write up the story and see how it goes...you never told me your name, by the way."

"I don't intend to." I grabbed the Gauguin, "Come here Archie. We're leaving." Archie followed me reluctantly as I stomped out of the office.

As we left, Gordon was typing away again, "Gauguin was a wife beater you know," he shouted after me without looking up.

"Even when you tell the truth, things don't work out," I said to Archie, who was sulking because he hadn't managed to eat all of Gordon's biscuits before we left.

I drove off fast, back to the forest and finally reached the place where we'd left our leopard. I was feeling nervous. Our leopard might be in a mood. Me and Archie got out of the car cautiously and walked round the car keeping our backs to it so our leopard couldn't creep up on us. But there was no sign of him. I looked up to the tops of the trees, hoping to see our leopard asleep with his legs draped over one of the high branches, but there was nothing. Gradually, we ventured further and further away from the car. There was a rancid smell of decay in the air. Archie put his nose to the ground and led me to a half-eaten deer.

"Leave it alone! It's disgusting," I said, grabbing hold of Archie, who was about to help himself to a leg or two. I pulled him away and had to drag him all the way back to the car and put him in the front seat. He barked at me and I wondered if he was challenging my authority, which is very unlike him – he's a very amiable dog and he doesn't like upsetting me. I looked him straight in the eye and he barked again and his eyes and ears went into his *I've heard something* mode.

43

I stood still and listened and heard the drone of cars in the distance, "Cars. You think they coming this way?" He gave me a look of infinite tolerance – that's another reason why he's my friend.

I jumped into the car and I drove through the trees as far away from the half-eaten deer as I could. The car bumped along until we came out onto the lane, just ahead of a line of cars. In my mirror, I saw someone stick their head out a car window and yell something at me.

I ignored them and drove on at high speed until we were on the other side of the forest where I parked the car amongst the trees.

We got out of the car and paced about. There was no doubt about it. They were on to our leopard and I bet some of them had guns. I could only hope that our leopard would outwit them all or be fast asleep up a tree somewhere and sleep through the whole thing.

I heard the approach of a large vehicle. The best I could do was to send it in the wrong direction, so I dashed out into the middle of the lane and started waving my arms about. Archie joined in by barking and throwing himself into the dog's version of a pirouette. A TV van screeched to a halt and a man leaned out of the window, "You two trying to get yourselves killed!"

"Wrong way! The leopard went that way," I ran round to the side of the van, "I've just seen it."

"Thanks, I'll tell the others." He was on his phone immediately. I backed away as he was saying, "It's this way...a woman's just seen it...yes...yes..."

Me and Archie were soon in the car and driving out of the forest. I had a plan now and was feeling quite cheerful. Archie wagged his tail – he knows when I'm happy – he's a very sensitive dog.

My plan went like this – a series of false leopard sightings would draw the hunters further and further way from our leopard until they got tired of it all and finally forgot him. Then, when it was all quiet, me and Archie would find him and coax him into the car and book a plane and fly him first-class to a leopard sanctuary in Africa – probably Kenya where there's plenty of long grass – and it would all be paid for by the sale of the Gauguin on the black market.

Now I knew Gauguin was a wife beater, I didn't want his painting, anyway, and would be glad to get rid of it and put it to good use. Me and Archie realised my plan was a romantic ideal but we were going to stick with it and so we set off for the nearest town to start spreading rumours.

We passed a sign saying *B&B with river views 1 mile on left.*

"We could stay the night and start a rumour," I told Archie, who wagged his tail, probably because he was expecting biscuits.

I stopped outside the B&B and rang the door bell – it had a cheerful chime but a mean looking woman with thin lips, answered it.

"Any vacancies?" I asked.

"How many?"

"Me and my dog."

"Sorry. No dogs allowed," she started to close the door.

"By the way," I said, "I've just seen a leopard swimming down the river. I'd keep inside if I were you."

"Are you sure?" Her mean eyes widened.

"Positive. I'm off to report it now." And with that I turned round and went back to the car. I heard her slam the door behind me.

"No dogs allowed. Don't take it personally, Archie, it's me she doesn't like." Archie wagged his tail – he appreciates knowing where he stands.

I drove off into the town centre. It was the ideal place to spread rumours so, when I stopped at some traffic lights, I opened the passenger window just as the lights turned green and Archie stuck his head out and barked to get attention and then I leaned over and stuck my head out and yelled, 'Just seen a leopard swimming down the river.' Some people stood still and glared, some laughed, and some pretended we weren't there at all and kept on walking. We did this at the next set of traffic lights and the next and the next, and by this time Archie was really enjoying himself and would have liked to carry on spreading rumours all day but I reckoned we'd told enough people, so I drove out of the town and headed for the coast.

We found a sleepy place with a mini-market, a craft cooperative, a gift shop and a newsagents with a billboard outside saying: LEOPARD SPOTTED IN SCOTLAND. IS IT A HOAX? The rumour was spreading fast and it was time to relax a little. I parked the car, then, me and Archie walked to the mini-market where I bought some proper dog food for Archie – which disappointed him – after being a free-wheeling scavenger of biscuits, it was a real letdown. I bought myself a healthy salad and a bottle of real fruit juice –

which disappointed me – Archie's not the only one who likes biscuits.

We walked out of the village and had a picnic on the beach. I imagined our leopard coming towards us across the sand – his greenish-golden eyes shining in the sunlight –his beautiful spotted body moving casually along in fluid motion.

"A leopard strolling along a beach. Could be our next rumour, Archie?" He wagged his tail, which is a sure sign he agrees with me, so we went back into the village and dashed into the newsagents as though a leopard was after us. The shop was small and crammed full of stuff. A miserable looking woman was serving from a counter squeezed in behind a wall of crisps.

"Just seen a leopard on the beach!" I shouted and we dashed out before we got in deeper.

We ran back to the car. Where next? A city where a black market in fine art flourished – where I could sell the Gauguin to the highest bidder. The nearest big city was Glasgow.

"Glasgow here we come!" Archie wagged his tail. He doesn't care where we go as long as he doesn't have to eat proper dog food and gets a biscuit or two.

We listened to the radio on the way. Our leopard was headline news along with wars and murders and miscarriages of justice.

"Several sightings of a leopard have been reported in Scotland. Our reporter Callum McIntyre has the details...

'It was here less than a mile from the village of West Kilbride that a leopard was reported to have been seen

47

wandering along this beach. Local police put out the following statement.

There's no evidence to suggest this is anything other than a hoax following on from earlier sightings south of the border and, while the public should not be alarmed by this latest possible sighting, we would urge anyone who does see what they think might be a big cat not to approach the animal, and to stay a safe distance away from it'...

*

I'd heard that Glasgow was the friendliest city in the UK as long as you *don't look at people the wrong way.* I'd also heard that Glaswegians were *violent, illiterate, partial to a good drink, football fanatics* and you couldn't understand a word they said and it was best not to wear orange or green in case someone tried to kill you for supporting the wrong team. Luckily, I've got no interest in football and Archie would join any team as long as they let him run after the ball now and again. Archie's not interested in prejudices – that's another reason why I like him. Me and Archie aren't interested in stereotypes either– we just wanted something to eat. So I parked the car in the centre of Glasgow and we set off to find food.

It was late but there were still quite a few people about who were obviously *partial to a good drink* so we avoided *looking at people the wrong way.* That's the trouble with stereotypes – some people do their best to live up to them. Eventually I asked a harmless looking young man where we could get something to eat.

Even though I quite possibly smelled bad because I hadn't had a wash for days, he replied, cheerily, "Well now you're asking. Let's see." And he actually trailed around Glasgow with us until he found an Indian restaurant where I bought a takeaway.

"Thanks very much for your help," I said.

"No problem, hen," he replied, "I'm a foreigner here too."

"Foreigner?"

"From Edinburgh," he laughed as he waved goodbye over his shoulder.

"By the way, I saw a leopard swimming down the Clyde," I shouted after him.

Several people turned their heads and laughed. He stopped for a moment and shouted back, "Aye, some people will believe anything."

Me and Archie went back to the car and I ate the takeaway while Archie stared at me until finally I gave him half my nan bread.

We fell asleep in the car and didn't wake up until the next morning when a policeman banged on the car window and set Archie off barking and growling.

I opened the car door and got out. The policeman stepped back as the smell of leopard mixed with curry wafted out of the car.

"Phew! What's that smell?" he sniffed in disgust.

"Leopard", I smiled at him, "and curry."

He raised his eyebrows, "This your car?"

"Yes."

"What you doing here?"

"I drove up from England yesterday. Arrived too late to find anywhere open," I said.

"Umm." He looked me in the eye, "Are you English?"

"Yes."

"Can I see your driving licence?" He was still looking me straight in the eye.

"Sorry, I don't have it with me," I said and expected him to arrest me on the spot and then search the car and find the Gauguin and put Archie in a home for mistreated dogs.

"Emergency! Come on!" A second policeman shouted from the open door of the police car parked in front.

"Ok! I'm coming!" The first policeman yelled back."Next time, have your licence with you", he said to me, "and move your car before nine o'clock or you'll have to put money in the meter."

"That was close," I said to Archie, as they drove away with their lights flashing.

It was then that I decided we had to get cleaned up. A stinking car wouldn't win us any favours, and me and Archie didn't smell too good either. You can get away with a lot if you're clean and tidy, and I had a feeling I'd need to get away with a lot when I was trying to find a buyer for the Gauguin on the black market.

I decided to get my car cleaned first. I drove around the city in search of a car cleaning place and ended up in Govan. I'd heard about Govan shipyards but I didn't see any ships. I stopped by a bus stop where several people were waiting.

"Is there a car cleaning place around here?" I shouted from the car.

"First on the right, best place in town," a man in overalls and heavy boots shouted back.

"Thanks very much. Lovely weather," I called out.

"Won't last," replied an old woman smoking a cigarette.

"Saw a leopard swimming down the Clyde!" I yelled to them as I drove off. I just couldn't resist spreading the word, after all, it was part of our plan and I wanted to feel a sense of progress.

"It'll all end badly," the old woman shouted after me. In my mirror, I saw her toss the butt of her cigarette to the ground and stamp on it.

A shiver went down my spine. I hoped she wasn't right. Just because a shiver goes down your spine, it doesn't actually mean anything, does it? Was it a prediction of our leopard's fate? A sad ending? An ending where the possibility of something wonderful was squashed like her cigarette. Fortunately, at this point I spotted the carwash place. A sign said, *Car Cleaned Inside and Out Only £20.*

Several cars were already being washed by young men dashing around with hoses.

As I got out of the car, Archie squeezed past me and, before I could stop him, he started prancing about in front of the hoses and laid down on his back with his legs in the air while they hosed down his stomach. I guess even dogs have a dirt tolerance limit. He caused quite a stir and the owner came out.

"Sorry about him. Any chance of cleaning my car, inside and out?"

He was a small lean man with a sense of purpose. He opened my car door and looked inside and quickly drew back, "What you had in there?"

"A leopard", I said, "and curry."

He laughed, "Smells like it. It'll cost thirty pound to get that clean and that's not counting the outside. Fifty pound and we'll do it now and your car will look and smell like new."

I didn't believe the *like new* bit but agreed to the fifty pounds because I had to get it cleaned up fast.

"Ok," I said opening the boot and taking the Gauguin out.

"You paint that?"

"Uh... yes, I'm thinking of selling it."

"Not much call for paintings round here. You should try Edinburgh."

While my car was getting a thorough makeover, Archie lay down and watched and I went inside to search for the toilet. I took the Gauguin with me.

The owner was at the desk on the telephone. He guessed I was looking for the toilet and pointed to a door at the back of the office. The toilet was brand new with gleaming white tiles and a large mirror next to the sink, so I got a full length view of myself. I looked much dirtier and messier than before. I washed my hands and face and ran my fingers through my hair but I still needed a makeover. The Gauguin looked even brighter in the white surroundings. I couldn't walk around with it tucked under my arm like this. Someone might recognise it – a passing policeman or an art critic or a discerning billionaire...

"Just popping up the road to buy some wrapping paper," I said to the owner on my way out.

Me and Archie walked down the street until we came to a corner shop, *Open All Hours*. An Asian man stood behind the counter watching my every move. I couldn't blame him – I looked like the shop-lifting type.

"Do you have wrapping paper and sellotape?" I asked sweetly.

"Third shelf on the left," he said in a Glaswegian accent – his relatives probably came here two hundred years ago.

I chose tartan wrapping paper because I'm in Scotland, after all, and went to pay with my card.

"Sorry. Over twelve pounds only," the man said.

"I'll buy something else then," I said. "Could you hang on to this while I look."

"No problem. Nice colours," he said when I handed him the Gauguin.

I wandered round the shop and chose five packets of digestive biscuits (mostly for Archie) and two packets of chocolate biscuits (for myself) and a big bottle of water and took them over to the till. It all came to thirteen pounds and fifty pence. Archie was wagging his tail a lot because of the biscuits.

"Can I wrap it up here?" I asked when the man passed the Gauguin back to me.

"No problem," he was smiling now.

After I'd wrapped up the painting, me and Archie sauntered out of the shop and made our way slowly back to the car wash and ate a whole packet of digestive biscuits while we waited.

"That's it finished," the owner said. He led us over to the car and opened the door with a flourish," Smell that!"

I stuck my head in the car and it smelt of roses and was really clean, "It's like new!"

"Said it would be. Didn't I?"

He was suspicious of my credit card when I paid, but it went through fine.

Archie got in the car and sniffed, disapprovingly, as we drove off in our like-new car with not a hint of leopard about it, which was rather sad and brought us down to the level of the ordinary and I remembered what the old woman had said and a shiver went down my spine again.

"Now it's my turn," I said to Archie who was still staring at the packets of biscuits.

I drove into the city centre and parked in a multi-storey car park.

"Stay. I'll be back soon," I told him.

*

I reappeared two hours later with bags full of new clothes and a new pair of expensive high heeled black and white shoes.

"Now we're off to a hotel," I said.

I parked a few streets away from the first hotel we passed.

"Stay. I'll be back soon." You could tell Archie didn't believe me.

I walked back to the hotel and went in carrying my shopping-spree bags and straight past the reception desk, with an air of confidence, and down a corridor. I tried every door and eventually found an open one and crept inside cautiously, "Hello."

"Hello," a woman's voice replied.

"Sorry, wrong room," I stepped back and ran down the corridor, turned left and bumped into a cleaner standing by an open door.

"Sorry," she said, "It's past checking-out time. You shouldn't be going back in."

This gave me an opportunity. "Only be a second. Just need to use the bathroom," I said and walked past her into the room and straight into the bathroom with my shopping bags.

I had to act quickly. I stripped off my dirty clothes and shot into the shower. I was covered in suds from head to toe when I heard her banging on the door.

"Ok, I'm coming!" In a panic I threw on the bright green dress I'd bought and the expensive high heeled black and white shoes and stuffed my dirty clothes and trainers into the shopping bags.

"Sorry about that," I said as I squeezed past the cleaner, ran down the corridor and out of the building. I was breathless by the time I reached the car. Archie was curled up asleep. Obviously, he wasn't expecting me to be back so soon and was still yawning as I drove off with my hair full of soap suds.

"Next stop hairdressers," I said screeching to a halt outside a salon called *Snipit by Emma*.

"What happened to you?" A small, thin woman with bright red hair, tied up in a spiky ponytail asked when I went in.

"Practical joke," I lied." It's just soap suds. Can you do anything with it?"

55

"Cut, wash and style for forty pounds," she said.

"That's fine. Go ahead and do it," I said.

"Are you Emma?" I pointed to the name on the window as I sat down.

"No, I'm Clare. I'm thinking of changing the name to *Clare's Hair*."

"That's much better," I said, even though it wasn't.

"You here on holiday?" she asked as she washed my hair.

"Business mostly."

"What sort of business?"

"Selling...on my way to sell a picture in Edinburgh. Got to look my best."

"Edinburgh's not like Glasgow, you know. They're all snobs. Come and sit over here." She wrapped my head in a tight turban and led me over to a chair,"About an inch off? What d'you think?"

"Fine." I was deep in thought about our leopard and was just about to say, *I saw a leopard swimming down the Clyde* – so she'd spread the rumour to her customers – when I realised that if I told her now she'd start asking all sorts of questions and would probably make a mess of my hair because she wasn't concentrating. I decided to spread the rumour just as I was leaving.

*

"That's it done. What do you think?" She showed me the back of my head with a mirror.

Scruffy grubber to city slick. Transformed. No sign of leopard about me. Back to my old advertising self. City slick success. "It's good," I said.

When I was paying with my credit card I said, "It's hard to believe someone saw a leopard swimming down the Clyde, isn't it?"

Why did I say *someone* saw a leopard? Why didn't I say *I* saw a leopard? Was I losing sight of my plan? Forgetting our leopard.

"Well a friend of mine saw a whale swimming down it once. If I saw a leopard swimming down the Clyde, I'd sell the story to the newspapers. You're the first customer I've had today. I could do with the money..." she hesitated and then exclaimed, "that's not such a bad idea!" She was already on the phone as I closed the door behind me.

It's called the law of unexpected consequences.

*

An hour later, I parked the car in the centre of Edinburgh and set off with the Gauguin tucked under my arm. Archie had to stay behind because he didn't fit in with my new image.

I'd never sold anything on the black market before and nobody has signs out saying *Black Market Deals Here*. But I thought a good place to start would be antique shops, so I went into the first one I came to. A tall thin man with wispy white hair and pale, unhealthy skin stood unsmiling behind a counter.

"I'm interested in selling a painting? I wondered..."

"Let's have a look," he interrupted impatiently.

Me and my Gauguin deserved more respect so I said, "Perhaps not," and walked straight out again.

Next I came across an *Antique Maps and Books* shop.

"Can I help you?" asked a small fat man with a pink face. He was smiling, which was an improvement on the last place, at least.

"I'm interested in selling this painting," I said.

"Sorry maps and books only but I know someone who might be interested. Is it by a well known artist?"

"Quite well known," I replied, carefully unwrapping the Gauguin and holding it up for him to see.

"A copy of a Gauguin. Tahiti. Pretty. How much do you want for it?"

"Thirty thousand pounds," I replied immediately, without thinking.

"Thirty thousand pounds! You've got to be joking!"

"No," I said. "It's thirty thousand pounds or nothing."

"It's nothing, then." And he turned to another customer who'd just come in.

I left and walked slowly up the hill. Obviously, I was going about it all the wrong way. Somehow, I needed to get in touch with the criminal underworld but I had no idea what a criminal from the underworld looked like.

"Haven't sold it yet have you?" someone whispered in my ear.

You have to be careful of people who whisper in your ear in the middle of a city. Ten to one they're from the criminal underworld.

I turned swiftly, "No." I was staring into the face of the tall thin miserable man from the first antique shop.

"The smiling one with the pink face. Don't trust him." And with that he walked off.

At this point, I decided I needed to see a friendly face so I headed for Archie and the car.

I got the feeling I was being followed and dashed down a narrow alley, which was a mistake. The alley led straight downhill becoming steep steps near the bottom, where I fell over and sprawled out right in front of a group of homeless people. The Gauguin went flying and landed in the middle of the road. It was going to be squashed for certain and the chances of funding a leopard sanctuary for our leopard were almost over.

It was then that the small fat man with the pink face dodged right past me as I lay there and came close to killing himself by dashing into the road and throwing himself protectively over the Gauguin. He obviously thought it was worth something.

I pushed myself up into a sitting position and staggered to my feet, with the help of one of the homeless young men, who was probably addicted to something and knew a bit about the criminal underworld.

I saw that the small fat man was running away with my Gauguin.

"Here. Have these!" I took off my high heeled shoes and thrust them at the young man, "They cost three hundred and five pounds."

I ran after the small fat man in my bare feet. I'm a good runner and I'd soon caught up with him and wrestled the Gauguin from his grip.

"So you do think it's worth something, then," I gasped breathlessly.

He was totally out of breath and even pinker in the face.

"I'll give you the thirty thousand," he managed to say.

"Hundred thousand to you!" I replied. I'd start high and maybe end up with fifty thousand.

"I'll have to check with my contact first. Bring it to the shop tomorrow...midday."

"Ok," I said and watched him limp away.

People were looking at me because of my bare feet, so I went into the first shoe shop I came to and bought a pair of trainers I could run fast in. Then I went into a Fish and Chip place and bought two Fish suppers and made my way back to Archie who was very glad to see me.

"You can come with me next time," I told him. "I may need you to bite someone." He was wagging his tail like mad, mostly because of the fish and chips.

We ate our fish and chips in the car and then I drove out of the city and parked down a lane. We got out and ran about in a field together. The only thing missing was our leopard. It wasn't the same without him.

We slept in the car down the lane and as soon as it was light set off for the city again. I parked the car in a supermarket car park and me and Archie and the Gauguin made our way to the *Antique Maps and Books* shop. It was midday when we walked into the shop.

The small fat man with the pink face ushered a customer out of the shop and locked the door.

"Can I look at it?" a tall man appeared from the back of the shop. He was wearing a suit and had white slicked-back hair contrasting with his black eyebrows. Obviously, the criminal underworld come in all shapes and sizes.

I carefully unwrapped the painting and held on to it as he looked at it through a magnifying glass.

"Where did you get it from?"

"Classified information," I said.

"You'll never sell it," he sneered.

I gave him a haughty look. I didn't like him at all.

"My dear, it's the genuine article. Nobody will touch it with a bargepole. Unless."

"Unless?"

"Unless I get a private collector interested. For ten percent."

"Ten percent of how much?"

"Shall we say a million?"

I tried to keep a steady, icy gaze, "Well a million is hardly enough to open a leopard sanctuary...they eat a lot."

"Leopard sanctuary?" He was the one looking surprised, "You're a conservationist then?"

"Me and my dog," Archie looked up at him, menacingly.

"I'll see if I can get more...there's no guarantee I can get anything. Give me a week. Shall we say meet here, same time next week."

"I'll try," I smirked and was out of the door in a flash, carrying the half wrapped Gauguin. We ran down the hill and round a corner until we were out of sight of the shop.

I was still shaking from the shock of the million pound offer when a drunk coming out of a pub shouted, "Hey you! You're the hoaxer!" before he staggered off down the cobbled street. People seem to get drunk early here – but why did he think I was a hoaxer?

61

We approached the pub door and I sidled in unnoticed with my back to the wall and told Archie to hide under a chair. The news was on the telly above the bar and it was all about leopard sightings. They'd been sightings all over the country. People telling lies to get in the limelight. They replayed a clip of a suspected hoaxer and it was a hazy video of me and Archie dashing out of the newsagents. My hair looked a real mess.

"The police would like to speak to this person," the newsreader said.

"Archie come here," I hissed. He'd gone over to the bar and was staring at a man eating a packet of crisps. The man turned, saw me and looked down at Archie, and before he had time to realise who we were, me and Archie were out of there and running.

We ran all the way back to the car, jumped in and were off.

In a panic, I drove out of the city and kept driving south for miles until the road got quieter and I found a lane leading to a beach. I drove down the lane and parked near some sand dunes.

We walked up and down the beach, thinking about our next move. Now what? Should I hand myself in? Tell the whole truth. I'd tried that and it hadn't worked. And now I was going to be prosecuted for being a hoaxer. I'd probably get six months and Archie would be impounded! But in a week I might have a million pounds and we could flee to Africa with our leopard. But in a week our leopard might have been spotted for real and shot! I'd set the whole country on the lookout – the rumour had worked too well. I had to stop the rumour and stay out of prison until I got the million pounds and we could flee to Africa.

"Come here Archie!" he was running up and down the beach, chasing seagulls.

I drove into the nearby town and parked outside the library and switched on my phone for the first time since leaving home. It was jammed full of messages. I deleted them all before they could suck me in and took a photo of the library and sent the photo with a message – *I am the hoaxer outside library in Scotland #leopardhoax.*

Then, I switched off my phone and waited.

It took half an hour before a TV van screeched to a halt in front of us. Me and Archie got out of the car and went up to the van. An excited reporter jumped out.

"On air now!" a voice screamed.

"Are you the hoaxer?"

"Yep...made up the whole thing...about spotting a leopard in my garden, how he hid in a waste bin outside a supermarket, and hunted at night, eating rabbits and chickens and deer and made a den in the back of my car and swam down rivers..."

"But why invent this whole leopard thing? Didn't you realise it might frighten people?"

"Not really and that's all I'm going to say." With that, me and Archie ran to the car, jumped in and we were out of there at speed, before we got arrested for making a nationwide nuisance of ourselves and wasting police time.

I kept driving until I was out of Scotland and in the depths of Northumberland. Being in the limelight isn't all it's cracked up to be. It was much better when it was just me, Archie and our leopard.

We stopped at an isolated spot in the middle of a National Park. It was raining so we sat in the car and listened to the radio and ate a whole packet of digestives. The news came on and, after a short clip of me admitting I'd made up the whole thing, there was an interview with my boss.

' *"She'd not been herself...taking long lunch breaks...not interested in her work...she blamed it on a leopard..."*

"And your recent Leopard Spicy Choco bar advertisement? I understand you were paid quite a high sum for it by a certain well-known chocolate company. You've both been accused of cashing in."

"Nonsense. We'd thought of it long before all this happened." '

"Liar!" I shouted at the radio. Archie jumped up and started barking. He's a very empathetic dog.

It's typical of my boss to cash in. That twenty thousand he offered me has now gone up to fifty thousand.

' *"And now we've got Madeline Croxley, a psychologist, on the line...Hello Madeline."*

"Hello."

"What's your take on this? Why would a person make up a story like this?"

"Usually because there's something missing in their life. They could be suffering from Narcissistic Personality Disorder..."

"Perhaps you could explain the symptoms...briefly Madeline, if you would..."

"Well, people who are narcissistic have to be the centre of attention...they seek admiration...they have

grandiose beliefs and spotting a leopard wandering about... well, it gets you noticed."

"Certainly does! Is Narcissistic Personality Disorder common?"

"Affects one percent of the population and it's on the increase...in Western societies."

"And I think the Greeks were the first to come up with it. Am I right?"

"Yes, Narcissus, the mythological Greek youth, fell in love with his own reflection in a lake. When he realised it was his own reflection, he died of grief because he'd fallen in love with someone who didn't exist outside himself."

"So he came to a bad end. Do you think the leopard sightings will go on, or, now that Lily Copley has admitted she started the whole thing, will that be the end of it?"

"Most likely the sightings will get less but you must remember that there are over two thousand sightings of big cats every year."

"Two thousand! And, I suppose the question is, are these big cats real or do people just make up the whole thing...a form of mass hysteria?"

"There may be big cats out there but it's much more likely that it's a deep seated fear, or a need for excitement, even danger, or the need to be noticed, as in the case of Lily Copley."

"That's all we have time for now. Thank you very much Madeline. That was Madeline Croxley, a psychologist, from Manchester and now for the weather. Rain..." '

I switched off the radio at this point. There *was* missing something in my life. She was definitely right about that. I was missing our leopard!

"Let's go and find him!" Archie wagged his tail – he's all for a bit of action.

*

When we were driving through a town, a police car drew up alongside us at some traffic lights and the driver stared at me. I thought he was about to recognise me so I turned left straight into someone's driveway.
Unfortunately, the door opened and a man with a shaved head stood there frowning at me. I opened my window.

"What d'you think you're doing?" he shouted.

"Sorry, wrong house," I smiled sweetly and backed out quickly.

It's difficult lying low when you look like me but the man's shaved head had given me an idea. I could get my hair shaved off and buy a wig with long straight hair and, with me in disguise, me and Archie would have a better chance of lying low. But the disguise would have to wait, because our leopard was waiting and he didn't care what I looked like.

*

It was getting dark when we got to the part of the forest where we'd last seen our leopard. It wasn't a good time to meet him. He'd be in hunting mode and, if he hadn't caught any deer recently, me and Archie might be good substitutes – especially if he was bearing a grudge because we'd deserted him. I parked the car among the trees and opened the back door and waited. Archie wandered about and barked a few times before he got back into the front seat and went to sleep. We woke up as soon as it was light and there was still no sign of our leopard on the back seat. We set off into the forest in search of him. Archie kept his nose to the ground. I kept my eyes on the tree tops.

Not a sign of our leopard. He might not be in the country any more. He might have gone on an island-hopping adventure and ended up in the Outer Hebrides, which isn't very likely, I thought, but just possible.

We gave up and went back to the car. As we got nearer, we got excited because he might be in the back seat having an afternoon nap.

We looked in hopefully. No sign of our leopard. We sat in the front of the car pondering our next move. I switched on the radio for a news update.

' *"We have unconfirmed reports that a leopard was shot this morning on the M6 just outside Holmes Chapel. It was seen wandering along the outside lane in a dazed and starving condition and may be the leopard sighted in recent weeks..."* '

I didn't hear the rest. I slumped down in the front seat and sobbed. They'd shot our leopard! It had all ended badly just like the old woman said it would. And he'd been dazed and starving. Me and Archie should never have left him. He must have walked miles searching for us. It was all my fault! The first time I saw him I should have reported him to the police. But they might have shot him right there and then and, at least, this way he'd had a few extra days eating rabbits and deer. But that didn't help much and I kept on sobbing.

And, after all, he wasn't a person, he was an animal. But that didn't help much either. I looked across at Archie, who was wagging his tail, which wasn't appropriate in the circumstances, but he's only an animal and doesn't know any better. Or does he? I stopped sobbing and sat up and looked at him closely. Perhaps he has a sixth sense and knows something I don't.

I started listening to the radio again,' *"an eye witness said he saw the leopard being carried away and driven off in a van..."* '

"Maybe it's not him? Is that what you think?" I asked Archie. I wish dogs could talk.

We had to find out for certain if it was our leopard and it might take longer than a week but the million pounds could wait.

*

We drove through the night, across country, down the M6 and got into Holmes Chapel just as the sun came up. But I got the feeling that the town wasn't the sort of place where a leopard, even a dead one, would feel comfortable. We passed a Vet's. Could that be where they'd taken the body? I parked the car down a side street and got out and looked through the window. All I could see was a waiting room and it didn't look big enough for our leopard. It was the sort of place where people took dogs and cats and rabbits and the occasional guinea pig – a leopard would be totally out of place there.

If we were going to find out where the leopard's body was, I'd have to ask questions and if I asked questions I'd be recognised and so would Archie. We had to get disguised and quick. Archie is a golden colour and dyeing him would be even harder than having a leopard in the back seat of your car. Disguising myself would definitely be easier – I could get my head shaved at a back street barber shop where people didn't ask too many questions, and then buy a wig or two.

I walked down several streets and found a barber's where it said, *Walk-ins Welcome*. It opened at nine so I went back to the car and decided to take a nap until it opened.

The traffic warden woke me up at nine and said I had to put the money in the meter *or else.*

It'll have to be the *or else* – I've only got my credit card and it's an old fashioned meter. I told Archie to stay and I'd take him for a walk later and set off for the barber's.

I was their first customer.

"Any chance of getting my head shaved. I'm in a play in Manchester this afternoon. Said I need to be bald for the part and I've got to leave in ten minutes!" I'm getting better and better at this.

The young man, who was attractive with dark brown eyes and a fancy beard, stared at me and I was just about to escape, because I thought he'd recognised me, when he said, "I can do that. Think I've seen you in something on the telly."

"Probably," I said hoping he didn't ask any awkward questions.

Luckily, because he only had ten minutes, there was no time to talk and he got to work immediately and I was soon bald and looked terrible.

"I look terrible. Do you sell wigs or can I buy that cap?" I pointed to a baseball cap hanging on the clothes stand.

"No wigs, sorry...take the cap. Think they sell wigs about three miles away...keep going down the main road. That'll be ten pound. What play are you in?"

I ignored the question, "Take thirty," I said, paying with my credit card, and grabbed the cap and stuck it on and was out of there and heading for the car.

I had a parking ticket – it blew away in the wind as I drove off.

I found a shop with a sign in the window saying, *Enjoy a new look instantly,* so I went in with the baseball cap pulled right down over my face.

"Need a new look, instantly", I muttered to a smiling face belonging to a substantial middle-aged woman with a fine head of black hair, "and it's urgent...got to be in Chester in an hour." I took off the baseball cap with a dramatic sweep. She just kept on smiling. Guess she'd seen a lot of bald heads in her time.

"Wedding is it?"

I nodded.

"The number of people who come rushing in here at the last minute. Now do you want long or short and the colour? Take a look at these while I measure your head," she handed me a catalogue.

I chose three wigs with enticing names.

"I'll have a long-dark-chocolate-henna-red and a long-cappuccino and a short-Swedish-blonde...just in case."

"Just in case?"

70

In case I have to change my identity at a moment's notice, "In case I change my mind when I get there," I said out loud.

"Well, if you're sure. Don't you want to try them on first?"

"No time," I said."

She hurried through a side door and was soon back with four wigs. She held them up for me to look at, "If you don't mind me saying, I think the Swedish-blonde will contrast with...with your face too much...why not have this autumn-mist instead."

"No. I'll take the Swedish-blonde."

Her smile wavered only for a second, "You could wear one of them now. What about the dark-chocolate-henna-red?"

She pulled the wig over my head and instantly I had dark-chocolate-henna-red flowing locks to hide behind.

I paid with my credit card and hoped it would go through ok – spending three hundred and forty six pounds on wigs isn't what I usually do. I guess the woman trusted me because I was bald or because, with my dark-chocolate-henna-red wig on, I looked like a film star or because it's Cheshire and she thought I was a footballer's wife going around spending money willy-nilly.

Archie barked at me when I got into the car and took a bite at the wig and pulled it right off my head. "Stop that! I'm in heavy disguise!" So much for being a film star.

"It's going back on," I told him, pulling it down tight over my head.

Archie was obviously suffering from being stuck in the car for hours so I drove down a farm track and we got out and ran about in a field and my wig didn't blow off in the wind.

We forgot about our leopard for a few moments but, once we'd stopped running, a shiver went down my spine and I remembered what the old woman had said and I realised that our leopard was probably dead and our search couldn't end well and I'd go back to work and refuse the twenty thousand pound pay-off – because it's more sensible to have a worthless job paying a regular amount each month. And they'd have to have me back – if they didn't, I'd take them to court – but I'd have to start again at the bottom of the ladder because Daisy had taken my job. And the leopard, the Gauguin, the million pounds and the leopard sanctuary would gradually become ancient history and people would talk about me behind my back...*she went mad...said there was a leopard in her back garden and it had a den in her car...*

I started to sob. Archie looked up at me reproachfully – he's no quitter and he doesn't expect me to be one either and anyway I'd just bought three wigs, surely I wasn't going to let them go to waste.

I blew my nose and was just wondering what to do next when a farmer came along on a tractor and started sounding his horn. My car was blocking his way and he had a big scowl on his face. I knew what he was thinking – *bloody foreigner.*

We ran back to the car and moved it to the side and the tractor just about scraped past and then slowed down and I think the farmer was going to get out to tell us off, so I quickly turned the car round and drove away – disguised by my long-dark-chocolate-henna-red wig.

"We'll have to find out as much as we can about the leopard shooting," I said to Archie. Archie wagged his tail in relief – he dislikes sobbing.

The best place to get information is a small corner shop which sells practically everything including newspapers and sausage rolls...but it's a bit of a corner shop wasteland around here.

I drove around in circles until finally I found one and went in and bought a chocolate bar, five packets of digestives, sausage rolls (for Archie), milk, oranges, apples and two cheese and tomato rolls, and I reckoned it would come to more than twelve pounds, so I could pay with my credit card.

The woman who served me was overweight and had dyed blonde hair – now I'm part of the wig wearing world, I could tell it wasn't a Swedish-blonde wig.

"Where did they take the leopard they shot yesterday?" I asked her.

"Back to the big house. He's got a zoo in there nobody knew about. He'll get prosecuted. Serves him right," she said.

"Is he going to make a rug out of the skin or something?" I was losing hope.

"A rug? The leopard wasn't dead. They shot it with one of those tranquillizer guns...heard it just now on the news."

"Not dead?!" I shouted.

"Nearly dead, they said, but not dead. Poor thing. Mind you I wouldn't like to meet it down a dark alley," she laughed.

I felt so cheerful, "You'd probably get eaten. Leopards hunt at night and drag the body up into a tree."

"Never get my body up a tree," she laughed loudly.

I skipped out of the shop, laughing all the way to the car.

Either, Archie was very pleased to see me so happy, or, he was looking forward to eating the sausage rolls.

I told him that, if it was our leopard, he was *alive* and now all we had to do was sneak into the Stately Home and see if it really was him. Archie was wagging his tail like mad, mostly because of the sausage rolls.

"You'll have to wait for your sausage roll," I said as I started up the car. It was obvious he didn't understand because he was still wagging his tail.

I drove straight past the driveway of the Stately Home and parked the car down a lane, leaving plenty of space for a tractor to pass. Then, I changed into the jeans and blue jumper I bought in Glasgow and set off on foot with Archie in the lead.

We reached the driveway and kept ourselves hidden by walking behind the shrubs at the side until, eventually, the drive opened up onto a lawn and behind the lawn stood the Stately Home, where, I was pretty sure, I wouldn't be welcome – especially if they thought I was a footballer's wife. Archie would be welcome, though, because he looks like a golden Labrador, even though he isn't.

"We're looking for leopards, remember," I whispered to him as we ran fast across the lawn and round to the back of the house. It was very quiet until we heard a noise like someone sawing wood and we knew straight away it was a leopard roaring. We gradually made our way towards the sound, through a vegetable garden and under an archway into a walled garden where there was an enclosure. The roaring was coming from a large, luxury hut painted blue and green.

We heard someone approaching.

"Archie come here. Now," I called out. He knows when I mean it and came running back to me. I grabbed hold of his collar and we lay flat on our stomachs in a flower bed.

A man dressed in overalls, carrying a large chunk of raw meat, came into the walled garden. Archie sniffed the air and tried to get free but I gave him a look and held on to him tight. We watched as the man went into the enclosure and straight into the hut. The roaring stopped and moments later the man backed out of the doorway still holding the meat and we caught our first glimpse of greenish-golden eyes. My heart leapt with joy – Archie had his nose in the air sniffing the meat.

The man tempted the leopard further and further out. Was it our leopard? Did I want it to be our leopard? Or did I really want it to be just another leopard – who happened to be living in someone else's back garden and had wandered off one night and ended up starving on the M6 in the fast lane? This leopard was all hollows with bones sticking out and it wobbled unsteadily on its feet and its spots were different. The man took a knife out of his pocket and cut off small pieces of meat and fed them to the leopard and stroked the leopard's head. The leopard began to purr. If this was our leopard, he'd found his way home, and he'd never been ours in the first place – he'd just been on a big adventure, got into a whole lot of trouble and was now back home being fed best steak by hand. Archie thought it was best steak too because he let out a bark of frustration at not getting any. The man turned round and saw us and the leopard snatched the rest of the meat out of his hand and slunk back into its luxury apartment. That leopard's not as domesticated as it looks.

"It's ok Sally. It's ok," I heard the man say as I dragged Archie out of the walled garden. Sally is not the sort of name I'd give to a leopard but one thing's for sure IT'S A GIRL'S NAME! So that settles it. It's definitely not our leopard.

When we got back to the car, we celebrated by eating biscuits and sausage rolls – I ate the biscuits and Archie ate the sausage rolls. It was time to change my disguise. The man would have noticed my long-dark-chocolate-henna-red wig so I changed it for the long-cappuccino.

Shaving your head and wearing wigs isn't such a bad way to live. Archie didn't like it though. He took a snatch at the long-cappuccino and tried to leap out of the car window with it in his mouth. There's something about wigs that brings out the worst in him.

*

"Scotland here we come. Our leopard and a million pounds are waiting," I said to Archie, cheerfully. He wagged his tail languidly – he was exhausted and so was I. Luckily, we soon came to a hotel where we stopped and booked a room, even though no dogs were allowed.

"Don't worry I'll get you in, somehow," I told him."Keep your head down and don't bark."

76

The receptionist took my credit card and, surprisingly, it went through – my bank obviously thinks I *am* the sort of person to spend three hundred and forty six pounds on wigs.

I managed to get Archie in by a back door and we dashed up to our room where I flopped down on the bed and Archie curled up on the carpet, and we didn't wake up until the next morning when the cleaner opened the door. Archie barked and the cleaner shouted, "A dog!" and rushed off to get the manager, probably.

"Archie come!" We ran out of the room, down the back stairs and out to the car. Archie leapt into the front seat. I went back to the room and locked myself in the bathroom and took a shower and sang very loudly. Someone tapped on the bathroom door but I ignored it and by the time I got out there was no one about.

I went down to Reception to check out.

"Have you got a dog?" the receptionist asked.

"No, but there was one in my room this morning. I chased it out."

She looked at me with narrowed eyes and a thin-lipped curl of the mouth and gave me back my credit card without a smile or a thank you. Some people think that having a dog in your room is worse than waging war in the Middle East or maybe she didn't like the contrast between my long-cappuccino wig and my *face*.

"Have a nice day!" I sang out sweetly and swept out into the rain.

It rained all the way to Scotland, and, when we got to Scotland, it rained even more. Our leopard wouldn't like it. He wouldn't be able to lie in the long grass sunning himself.

I drove towards the Laughing Horse pub and listened to the news. There was nothing about leopards at all. They'd been pushed out of the breaking news by stories of tax dodgers and bank corruption. Things were looking up – just so long as our leopard didn't try to eat any people before I'd got the million for the Gauguin and set up a leopard sanctuary **and** emigrated to Africa with him.

At last, we arrived at the Laughing Horse. The young man with blonde hair and a full set of teeth recognised me and Archie immediately – so my disguise is practically useless. The bar was empty, which was a relief. I was too tired to put up with bigots.

"Fish and chips for you and a beef sandwich for him, is it?"

"Yep."

"What happened to your hair?"

"Shaved it all off," I whipped off my wig and showed him my bald head. I'm usually very sensitive about my hair style – I don't know what came over me. Could it have been a test of his devotion?

"Wow! Nice shaped head! My name's Graham by the way." He held out his hand.

I quickly put the wig back on and shook his hand. "Lily," I said."And that's Archie." Archie wagged his tail at the mention of his name."Ever been to Africa?" I asked to divert Graham's attention away from baldness and wigs.

"No. Why? You thinking of going?" He looked disappointed.

"Me and Archie are considering it. We're going to set up a leopard sanctuary."

"No kidding!"

"You can come with us if you like?" I smiled in a dubious sort of way so he could pretend it was a joke and turn me down easily.

"Love to but can't. No money. Why d'you like leopards so much?"

"Because they're beautiful." I didn't tell him it was really because a leopard turned up in my garden one day and, until then, I'd never even thought about them at all, and I didn't tell him about the Gauguin and the million pounds, either. He went behind the bar and into the kitchen to order our meal.

After we'd eaten our meal, I talked to Graham about sneaking a dog into a hotel room. Which was worse, to sneak a dog into a hotel room or to wage war in the Middle East?

He said, of course, on the face of it, it was far worse to wage war in the Middle East. But, then again, it probably depended on what experience you had. For example, if you had to clean up a room full of dog hairs and had no experience of wars and no interest in what was happening outside the hotel room, you'd probably think sneaking a dog into a hotel room was worse. I stopped him there, by saying that, surely, with even a mere scintilla of thought, a person must realise that waging a war is worse. He came back with, yes, but the dog hairs are real, whereas to some people wars are just news. I came in with, yes, in other words, most people are so caught up with the day to day trivia of their lives, they don't think past the dog hair problem and it doesn't say much for the state of our society. He agreed it didn't. Finally, we agreed it was definitely worse to sneak a dog into a hotel room *and* wage war in the Middle East and this made us laugh so loud that Ashar, the cook, came out of the kitchen to see what we were up to. But Ashar was actually born in the Middle East and didn't think it was funny, at all.

Me and Archie were sorry to leave the Laughing Horse. I was sorry because I liked talking to Graham and he isn't bad looking either and Archie was sorry because he likes the beef sandwiches.

"I'll call back when I've sorted out the money for the leopard sanctuary," I said.

"Look forward to it," he said and hugged me tight. Things are definitely looking up.

"Would you like to see my Swedish-blonde wig?"I said.

"Ok." He followed me out to the car where I swapped the long-cappuccino for the Swedish-blonde.

"Wow! Stunning," he said, "Why don't you keep it on?"

"I'm saving it." I said and put the long-cappuccino back on.

"For what?"

"A rainy day." Me and Archie got into the car.

"You don't have to shave your head to wear wigs, you know," Graham said."Why did you shave your head?"

He's getting very personal and obviously thinks I'm some sort of nut case who's into self humiliation. When really I'm just an inexperienced wig wearer and thought bald heads and wigs went together and it only just now dawned on me that I could have saved myself from baldness.

"Wig wearing is more comfortable when you're bald," I said, confidently, as though I was a world expert.

"You're probably right," he said and, as I shut the car door, he added, "Be sure you don't meet any leopards."

Did he know I was the leopard hoaxer? Had he seen me on the telly dashing out of the newsagents? I couldn't tell by his face – but, if he knows, he probably thinks I'm suffering from an unusual form of insanity and it's better not to ask too many questions until I'm ready to talk.

He stood outside the Laughing Horse and waved until we turned a corner.

"I'll miss him," I said to Archie. Archie looked glum. He was missing the beef sandwiches already. He's not really a Labrador but he acts like one.

We had three days to find our leopard before I picked up the million pounds in Edinburgh and, if the million pound deal didn't come off, we'd have to swim to a remote island with our leopard and live off the land. Except I'm not sure any remote islands actually exist around here.

It was still light when we got to the forest and immediately started hunting for our leopard. Archie sniffed the ground and I looked up into every tree. Once or twice I thought I saw his beautiful spots shifting through the leaves in the shadows but it turned out to be leaves and shadows. We searched until it was dark before we gave up and went to sleep in the car.

We were woken by a blackbird which annoyed Archie. As soon as I let him out of the car, he chased it away – if he had a birth certificate I could check how much of a Labrador he really is.

All that day we searched. Nothing. No sign. And the next and the next until it was time to drive to Edinburgh to collect the million pounds. Our plan was falling apart but we set off for Edinburgh, anyway, and went down all the small roads and lanes looking out for our leopard all the way. No sign. Nothing.

We got to Edinburgh late and parked below the castle and fell asleep in the car and, as long as we woke up early, we wouldn't get a ticket.

*

Archie woke me up by pulling off my long-cappuccino wig. I gave him a severe look even though he was right – we had to make an early start, especially if we wanted breakfast. We went for a walk through the quiet streets and found a small Italian cafe in Grassmarket. It had a notice on the door which said, *you must buy food with your drink,* which wasn't exactly welcoming but I went in anyway. The young woman serving was tall and thin with black hair tied back and an expression of acute impatience. She definitely needed a course in customer relations.

Archie was wagging his tail vigorously when I came out of the cafe with a bag full of sandwiches. We went back to the car and I ate a salad sandwich and Archie ate a ham sandwich. We'd only just swallowed the last bite when we saw the traffic warden approaching so I drove off to the same supermarket car park we'd been to before.

I left Archie in the car sleeping off his ham sandwich and went shopping. In a fancy upmarket department store I bought a black fitted suit, black high heeled shoes, a gold necklace and a large handbag to put the million pounds in. I kept on the suit and shoes and put my jeans and jumper in the fancy upmarket bag they'd given me. When I was leaving an assistant noticed me and accused me of stealing everything until I showed her the receipts.

Now I was ready to collect the million pounds off the white-haired man with black eyebrows from the criminal underworld.

Archie was still asleep when I got back to the car.

"You're coming with me," I told him. "You really might have to bite someone this time." He wagged his tail. He's never bitten anybody in his life but he knows when something exciting is going to happen.

I got the Gauguin out of the boot and we walked through the cobbled streets to the *Antique Maps and Books* shop. It was just after midday. It said *Closed* on the door probably because they had a million pounds in there. I knocked three times and the small fat pink-faced man opened it. I stepped inside and immediately I was surrounded by three men in balaclavas – one had green eyes and the other two had brown eyes.

"Archie bite them!" I screamed.

Archie's had no practice at biting but, once he'd bitten one of them, he seemed to get the hang of it and leapt about with his teeth bared and flung his big lump of a body at them, until he was causing chaos and the books and maps were falling off the shelves and the men's clothes were torn and my wig had fallen off.

The white-haired man with the black eyebrows suddenly appeared from the back of the shop,"Stop! Call him off! He'll bite the painting next!"

I shouted, "Down, Archie, down!"

Archie pranced around a few more times before coming to stand next to me. He was still growling like mad and I still had the Gauguin. "Where's the money?" I demanded.

"Here's the money! Now give me the painting!" The white-haired man thrust a plastic bag into my hand.

"I'll have to count it first."

"No time for that. Give it to me now or the deal's off."

Since Gauguin was a wife beater and the painting wasn't really mine and my wig had fallen off, I did as he asked, and gave him the Gauguin and backed out of the shop with Archie growling beside me. I left my cappuccino wig in the shop as a souvenir – I didn't really like that one as much as the others, anyway.

I walked down the hill as fast as I could in my high-heeled shoes, grasping the plastic bag, which was probably full of newspapers. Archie was quivering beside me – all that biting had upset him quite a bit. He threw himself into it at the time but it's not his style – he's a Labrador at heart, even if he hasn't got a pedigree.

Just in case the men in balaclavas were following us, I stepped quickly into an Indian clothes shop. The woman behind the counter gave me and Archie a pitying look and handed me a multi-coloured scarf.

"Take it. It's free." Obviously she thinks baldness suits some people more than others. I took it and

wrapped it round my head like a turban, "Wonderful,"
she said, "Beautiful!"

Was I more noticeable as a completely bald woman
in a black suit and high heels or as a woman wearing a
multi-coloured turban and a black suit and high heels?
There wasn't much in it and the only thing to do was to
get to the car in the fastest possible time and put on my
long-dark-chocolate-henna-red wig. I thrust my hand
into the plastic bag, in the hope that there may be a few
pounds in there I could give to the woman, and my hand
came out grasping a red bank note.

I was as surprised as the woman and, before she
could ask any tricky questions, I put it on the counter and
quickly stuffed the plastic bag into my new handbag and
dashed out of there.

"Yippee!" I shouted as we ran through the streets
back to our car and only a few people looked our way –
Edinburgh locals must be used to weird sights because of
the festival.

Once we were in the car, we felt safer and I calmed
Archie down by giving him some biscuits and I
exchanged the turban for the long-dark-chocolate-henna-
red wig, the suit for jeans and a red t-shirt and the black
high-heeled shoes for trainers. I'm getting expert at
changing in confined spaces.

Now to count the cash. I looked all around. There
were people going in and out of the supermarket but no
one who looked as though they might have been wearing
a balaclava ten minutes ago, so I took the plastic bag out
of the handbag and looked inside.

It was full of red notes. I took some out and
examined them. Scottish hundred-pound notes! I looked

inside the plastic bag again. It was full of them. Archie sniffed inside the plastic bag, searching for biscuits. He wasn't impressed. Maybe he was right – he knew these were fake Scottish hundred-pound notes and no use for buying biscuits.

We had to find out if they were fake and whether our plan to start up a leopard sanctuary in Africa was still on the cards, and the best way to do this was to take a couple of the notes to a bank. Banks can detect fraud at a hundred paces – mostly because they've had training in the deceptive use of other people's money.

"Stay Archie. I don't need you to bite anyone. I'm off to the bank." He looked relieved, curled up and went to sleep. He's had an emotionally draining afternoon.

I put two hundred-pound notes into my new handbag and locked the plastic bag full of the red notes in the boot and set off for the bank.

I headed for Princes Street and walked through an old churchyard on the way. There was some sort of incident going on in there. A couple of drunks were shouting loudly at two policemen and I thought I heard the word *leopard* mentioned more than once, but that's probably because I don't know where our leopard is and he could be anywhere and he could easily hide behind one of those gravestones.

I went into the first bank I came to.

"I've got two hundred-pound notes," I said to the young woman at the counter. "They were a present. I'd like to set up a savings account."

"No problem. Just fill in this form," she said and passed me a form.

I saw that the form asked for full name and address, "It asks for an address. Can I leave that out?"

"Sorry, no, and I'll need proof of identity."

I should have known that only banks are allowed dodgy dealing and there was no chance of me using a false name and address. It's called having one law for the cunning rich and another for the inexperienced seller of stolen Gauguins.

So I filled in the form using my real name and address, which felt uncreative but essential if I wanted to test if the notes were real or not. I passed the form back to the young woman and showed her my credit card. She entered my details into the system very slowly – I think it was her first day.

"That's fine. You're depositing two hundred pounds?"

"Yes, two hundred pounds." I handed over the two red notes and waited. I felt a bit shaky – after all, the leopard sanctuary and our trip to Africa were hanging in the balance.

She held the notes up to the light, "I'll be back in a minute." She disappeared through a door.

"That's fine. Your account is all set up," she suddenly appeared behind me and handed me a Paying-in book. I won't be paying anything in – I'm spending it on a leopard sanctuary.

I skipped out of the bank back to Archie. He was still asleep.

"We're rich," I said and he just kept on sleeping. Dogs are only interested in what money can buy, especially if it's biscuits. "But I don't know how rich we are."

I needed somewhere quiet to count the money so I drove round to the back of the supermarket where the bins were. As I passed the bins, I thought I saw our leopard's ears sticking out of one of them. But that's probably because I'm worrying about him.

I got out of the car to get the plastic bag full of money out of the boot and heard the sound of someone sawing wood. It was coming from behind the bins. I woke Archie up, "Listen to that!" His ears pricked up and then he went back to sleep again. There's leopards roaring and then there's people sawing wood.

I sat in the front seat and counted the money. It took ages especially because I had to keep looking up to check nobody was walking past with their shopping. I counted four hundred and ninety nine thousand and seven hundred pounds – so the white-haired man from the criminal underworld had kept half for himself and his accomplices and *he* didn't even get bitten by Archie. But, even though the Gauguin was a present from our leopard to me, it wasn't really mine, so I reckon we did quite well out of it.

All we had to do now was find our leopard and set off for Africa – which was such an impossible task I decided to take a break and find somewhere to eat. I took two hundred-pound notes out of the plastic bag and then hid the bag in the boot under the spare wheel and checked three times that I'd locked the car before we left.

We followed a pathway lined with trees leading away from the city centre and eventually came to the Water of Leith. Restaurants with tables outside lined the cobbled street and a sign said, *Enjoy an al fresco pint in the brief Scottish summer.*

"We deserve to enjoy ourselves," I said to Archie and sat down at one of the tables.

I ordered salmon and chips and salad and coffee and cakes and a pint and beef sandwiches to eat there and a whole cake to take away. I ate the salmon and chips slowly and Archie ate his beef sandwich in fifteen seconds flat. The bill came to thirty pounds and forty pence.

I handed over one of the hundred-pound notes to the waitress, who looked worried and hurried back into the restaurant. She was in there for quite a while. They were probably subjecting the hundred-pound note to all sorts of tests. Eventually, she came out with my change and a bowl of water for Archie. She was all smiles now – it's amazing what a difference money makes. I wonder what she would say if I put my Swedish-blonde wig on? Was she the sort of person who'd go back into the restaurant and tell her pals that it didn't suit my *face?* I'd never know, so I smiled back.

Me and Archie wondered off down the cobbled street and took a wrong turning and ended up near the Botanic Gardens. We passed a posh looking hotel and it said *Dogs Welcome.*

"We'll stay here for the night," I said to Archie. "We deserve it."

We strolled into the hotel and up to the reception desk.

"How much is it for one person and a dog for one night?"

"Eighty nine pounds."

"That's fine," I replied, which took the receptionist by surprise.

Our room was luxurious compared to anything and especially compared to sleeping in a car. I asked for a pot of tea to be sent up to our room and we ate our cake and washed it down with the tea.

I switched on my phone and phoned my mum and most of the conversation was about her being very worried about me. She said she'd phoned and phoned and always got the answering machine and my boss had phoned her and asked her if I was ill and then she'd heard me on the radio and it was obvious I was up to some advertising stunt because of the leopard hoax thing and the *Leopard Spicy Choco bar,* which had sold well and made my boss a mint, and in future, she said, I mustn't switch my phone off.

After that, she said I sounded happy and I said, well, yes, I was, but I just had a few things to sort out before I came back down South. She asked me where I was staying. I told her how posh it was and she said, how can you afford it, and I told her I'd been given a second hand painting by a friend and it turned out to be a masterpiece and so I'd got quite a lot of money for it and when I was back home she could have thirty thousand pounds to pay off her mortgage and she started laughing and shouting and said, "Are you **sure**", about fifty times. She asked who the friend was and was I going to share the money with them and I said, yes, of course I was going to share the money and it was someone she didn't know.

She asked how Archie was and I said he'd bitten a couple of people recently, who'd tried to steal the painting, and she said that wasn't like Archie at all. I agreed with her and told her it did take it out of him but we'd just had a huge meal and he'd had beef sandwiches and now he was eating a piece of cake so I thought he was totally recovered.

My mum knows a thing or two and obviously knew I wasn't telling her the whole truth. Before she rang off she said, "I know you're up to something, please be careful".

Archie loves my mum – she always gives him a biscuit when he goes round to her house and he's allowed to sit on her settee, which definitely isn't allowed in my house.

We fell asleep after that and woke early the next morning and walked back to the car to get some more money because we'd already spent almost two hundred pounds in one day, but there was plenty left. The money was still there hidden under the spare wheel and this time I took out ten hundred-pound notes, just in case.

I drove the car back to the hotel and booked me and Archie in for another two weeks because we needed a holiday after all we'd been through. I asked the receptionist if they had a dog walking service and she said, no, they didn't, but she'd get someone for me and when did my dog want to go out, exactly. I told her that Archie wasn't fussy as long as he got out because he didn't want to stay in while I was out shopping.

A young man with four dogs came round an hour later and Archie got very excited and jumped all over the other dogs, who were calm and collected compared to him. Archie went off for a walk in the park with them. He was wagging his tail furiously – he's glad to see the back of me for a while.

I had ten hundred-pound notes in my pocket and needed to change them into something less suspicious.

So I walked into the city centre and bought a pair of red sandals to go with my long-dark-chocolate-henna-red wig and the assistant accepted the note without even looking at it properly. After that, I had my toe nails and my finger nails painted white with little red flowers and diamonds and these looked good with the red sandals and with the red dress I bought later – the dress only cost three hundred and ninety nine pounds.

On the way back, I passed a dog pampering place where I booked Archie in for a session of *Exclusive Dog Grooming* and bought him a red collar studded with diamonds to go with my dress.

Archie was waiting for me at reception and was very glad to see me even when I put the red diamond-studded collar on him and he squirmed about and rubbed his whole body along the ground and tried to get it off. The receptionist said it suited him and he soon forgot it when she gave him a biscuit.

Then we had a slap-up meal in our room.

"You're going to be groomed tomorrow," I told him. It's probably a good job he doesn't understand.

The next day we had a five star breakfast before we went to the dog pampering place.

"Come back in an hour," the man said when I handed Archie over.

Archie looked very sad but we had our new image to live up to.

I wandered back to the car to check on the money and decided that the car definitely let our new image down. I'd only bought the car a year ago, but it was black and steady looking and what me and Archie needed was a red jaguar to go with his collar. I drove round looking for a Car Sales place.

The first one I came to didn't sell red jaguars and the only red car they had, that I could swap with mine and *drive away today*, was a hybrid BMW costing fifty thousand pounds and I said that it would have to do because at least it was red.

I haggled with the sales man, who looked up what my car was worth and said it was only worth forty thousand pounds and also it smelt a little and so I couldn't do a straight swap and would have to pay the difference in cash. I said that, if I had to do that, I'd pay by credit card and that was the deal, take it or leave it – and he agreed because I think he's a dodgy dealer and he knows he can get more for my car than forty thousand. He said he'd have to check with his boss though. And the boss came out and looked me up and down and said, he'd hoped he wouldn't regret it, but, yes, I could pay by credit card. So I said, fine, as long as he gave me the keys to the car first and signed it over to me. He's a polite dodgy dealer and said "Of course madam". I'm fairly sure he'd say my *face* didn't suit a Swedish-blonde wig.

While he was sorting out the paperwork, I emptied everything out of my old car and put it in my new car and, when I was sure nobody was looking, got the plastic bag full of money out from under the spare wheel and hid it under the front driver's seat of my new car.

An hour later, I parked my brand new red car outside the dog pampering place and Archie was really miserable because he smelt lovely and clean and had a fluffy look about him. At first, he wouldn't get into the car because it smelt too new but I persuaded him in with a biscuit.

The girl at reception was impressed with the bright red car and even more impressed by Archie – all spruced up and wearing his red, diamond-studded, collar. She definitely thinks me and Archie are film stars in disguise. She looks seventeen but she's probably twenty three.

We drove off in our brand new red car and arrived in a place called Cramond. Archie had a great time running up and down the promenade wearing his brand new red, diamond-studded collar and I walked along in my brand new red shoes and red dress and we looked a million dollars. We turned people's heads and got served like royalty when we stopped for a coffee. If I was wearing my Swedish-blonde wig, would the people here say it didn't suit my *face?* Now I'm rich, I've no way of telling. It depressed me a little. I needed a night out on the town and for that I needed a slinky dress and a diamond necklace.

"Let's go Archie," I called out to him and he followed me very slowly at a distance. He prefers the seaside to the hotel room.

We drove off in our brand new car and several people actually waved at us. I waved back in the way royalty do – they know a thing or two about maintaining their living standards by manipulation of the masses.

We got back to the hotel and I left Archie in the hotel room and set off on foot to buy the slinky dress for my night out on the town. After hours of trying on dresses, boredom set in. Spending loads of money isn't the same as having dreams.

Had I given up on my dream of finding our leopard, setting up a leopard sanctuary and emigrating with him to Africa? Spending money was so much easier. But how much money had I spent?

I rushed back to the hotel, got the plastic bag out of the car and went up to our room. Archie leapt at me as usual and made a grab for the plastic bag and ripped it in half. The notes flew about everywhere and Archie dashed around tearing them up and I started laughing and then felt really guilty because people were starving in some parts of the world and we were rolling about laughing in money.

"Stop it now!" I told him, "It's time to get serious!"

I collected up all the notes and placed them in one thousand pound bundles and the notes that were torn in half I put in another pile.

I'd spent over fifteen thousand pounds already not including the hotel bill and the thirty thousand pounds I promised my mum for her mortgage. Things had got to change.

"No more frivolous spending", I told Archie, "and that includes beef sandwiches."

The impossible task of finding our leopard had to be tackled head-on.

What would our leopard do when he realised we'd left him in the forest? First, he'd try to follow us. He could have run after the car down all those lanes and got to Glasgow and swum down the Clyde and followed us to Edinburgh and hidden in a supermarket bin and wandered into the dog pampering place...but this was ridiculous. Wasn't it?

Or he could have followed us some of the way and given up when he came across some chickens or a deer and stopped and had a feast and then spent several nights sleeping it off up in a tree, which was much more likely.

Or he could have looked up to the stars, worked out where he was and made his way home like a homing pigeon...to the long grass in my back garden!

"Come on Archie!"

I paid the hotel bill with my credit card but it was rejected so I paid with one of the hundred-pound notes and the receptionist took it as though she saw hundred-pound notes every day.

"Where you off to now?" she asked.

"Leopard hunting."

"In Africa?"

"Well...not quite...," I smiled and we were out of the building and into our brand new red car. The car was already getting messy with packets of biscuits lying about, so Archie didn't mind it as much.

I headed South and put the radio on to listen to the breaking news – tax dodgers, hacking, police misconduct, and it wasn't going to rain today – no mention of leopards at all, so our leopard had either been very cunning or big cat sightings weren't the favourite story of the week.

I drove for six hours straight and at last drew up in front of my house. It looked the same as when we'd left.

"Come on Archie!"

We ran round the house to the back garden and peered over the gate. We had to be careful. We didn't want to surprise our leopard and be eaten because he'd mistaken us for food.

We couldn't see a thing so I opened the gate and we went in but I knew our leopard wasn't there because Archie just wandered about aimlessly. Our hopes were dashed.

We went sadly into house by the front door. There was a pile of mail on the floor – letters from my bank and from my boss and from companies who specialised in sending out junk. Perhaps it's a mistake coming back.

*

The next day I leapt out of bed and rushed outside to see if our leopard had returned. Nothing. No sign.

What now? Put the money in a savings account a little bit at a time so that it wouldn't look suspicious? Go back to work? Forget about our leopard dream? I burst into tears. Archie looked at me in disbelief. He was right. Again, I was giving up too easily. The opportunities were endless – I just had to put the effort in.

First, we went to work. Archie doesn't usually come to work with me but this was a special occasion. He had on his red diamond-studded collar and I was wearing my Swedish-blonde wig and the red dress with the red sandals, and my nails were a bit chipped but they still looked good. We drove into the City in our brand new red car and we looked a million dollars.

I parked in the *VIP Visitors Only* spot and walked into the office with Archie at my heels, straight past Daisy, who was sitting at my desk, and into the boss's office.

"I'll take a hundred thousand pounds and leave without a fuss," I said.

He just stared at me until Archie barked and started sniffing around for biscuits.

"You're back," he stammered.

"I'm only here for the money...if it wasn't for me and the leopard hoax..."

"We've had to drop the *Leopard Spicy Choco bar* campaign...police said we were whipping up mass hysteria," he said quickly.

"Not before you'd made a load of money. Ok, if I'm not getting the money, I'll just stay." I stormed out of the office and over to my desk and Daisy jumped up out of my chair, mostly because Archie was giving her a look.

The office had gone very quiet until someone said, "Wow. You look fantastic. Good work with the leopard hoax. It was a marketing masterpiece. The chocolate people loved it."

The boss came out of the office waving a cheque in his hand, "Take it! Take it! And, if I see you and your dog in here again, I'll have you thrown out!"

I walked up to him, took the cheque out of his hand, with an extravagant flourish, and glided out with a big flashy smile on my face. I checked to see if Archie was following me and he swallowed something, guiltily. Someone had given him a biscuit.

When we were back in the car, I looked at the cheque – it was for fifty thousand pounds only, which was to be expected from such a mendacious ex-boss but it was more than enough to pay off my mum's mortgage.

Now I was jobless with a dog, a house, a car, and at least four hundred thousand pounds and dreams.

I gave my mum the thirty thousand pounds to pay off her mortgage and we all went out for lunch to celebrate. Afterwards, me and Archie went home to see if our leopard was back. Nothing. No sign. But we still had hope that he would be back soon so we continued with our plans only in a different order.

The most logical way forward was to find our leopard, then go to Africa, and then set up a leopard sanctuary. But there was nothing stopping us from setting up a leopard sanctuary first, was there? And by then our leopard might have turned up in my back garden.

As soon as I began to think seriously about setting up a leopard sanctuary in Africa, I realised it could just be a matter of popping into London Zoo and offering them four hundred thousand pounds and hey presto they'd do the rest for you or know somebody who could. It's amazing what you can do if you've got money.

But then there was the obvious problem of thousands of pounds in a hundred-pound notes – zoos would definitely be fussy about where the money came from. And they might be fussy about other things too, like preferring to help elephants, or rhinos, or dormice, for that matter...or penguins, or sharks, or bottle-nosed dolphins...and even insects might come into it...and leopards could be well down on their list and they would have a point. Why should leopards get special treatment just because one happened to turn up in my back garden one day?

I needed to talk it through with someone and the first person who came to mind was Graham from the Laughing Horse but he was too far away and the second person who came to mind was Archie but he's only a good listener, so I did the next best thing, which was to go to my local cafe where Sarah, the owner, is always full of opinions.

Sarah's a big woman, tall and broad. She used to work in a college, giving out advice and helping students with their housing and money problems and eventually helping anyone at all who turned up at her office, until, that is, she got overwhelmed with all their problems and gave it up to run a cafe, where she sells coffee and cakes and gives out down-to-earth advice for free.

I sat at a table near the counter so that I could talk to her when she wasn't serving customers.

"If you had about half a million pounds what would you do with it?" I asked.

"I'd give up this place and go travelling, see the wonders of the world," she spread out her arms and laughed. "By the way is that a wig you're wearing?"

"Yep, Swedish-blonde. Had my hair shaved off so I could wear it."

"You idiot! You don't have to have your hair shaved off to wear a wig!"

"I know. Didn't realise it at the time – I had to make a quick decision," I said.

"Yes, I'd heard you'd got yourself mixed up in some weird leopard drama. Less said about that the better, I expect," she gave me a wary, sideways glance. "The wig suits you, anyway," she sat down at my table. "If I had half a million, I'd have to think carefully for about...thirty seconds...and then go out and buy myself some new clothes and new shoes and a new house and a new car and then I'd buy myself a designer handbag costing four thousand pounds and then I'd give up this cafe and go travelling." She got up to serve a customer. I expect she thinks she's got a right to spend money on herself for a change.

She came back and sat down again, "Oh and I'd find myself a new man."

This wasn't getting me anywhere.

"What if you had thousands of pounds in Scottish hundred-pound notes? What then?"I said.

"Is this some sort of quiz?" she asked.

"Call it an intelligence test" I said.

"Call it money laundering," said a man in a suit at the next table.

"So it's stolen money. That's different. I'd get rid of it...quickly," she looked serious.

"Gradually feed it into your bank account or spend it bit by bit all around the country," the suited man advised.

You can always rely on men in suits to know what to do with dodgy money.

I tried another question. "Would you give the money to an animal sanctuary?"

"Definitely not...you mean donkeys?"

"Donkeys or leopards maybe?"

"What's wrong with people?" she said.

"Leopards are beautiful?" I said.

"Give it to the homeless...some of them sit in here all day and take up the tables...that'd be doing me a favour," she laughed and went back behind the counter.

I finished my coffee, "See you later."

"Remember the homeless!" she shouted after me.

*

I was following Sarah's advice and heading for Brixton in a taxi with Archie and one hundred thousand Scottish hundred-pound notes in a plastic bag.

An hour later the taxi driver dropped us off outside the only Community Centre he knew in Brixton.

We went in and two fierce looking dogs with half their ears missing rushed up to Archie, but he's used to dealing with a leopard, so he just sat down and didn't move a muscle until they got bored and wandered away. There were some teenagers loping around looking cool. A very tall muscular man came over to us, "You want something?"

"Are you in charge here?"

"That's me."

"I'd like to help the homeless of Brixton."

"Help? What d'you mean, exactly?"

"Well, I give you a hundred thousand pounds and you help the homeless and ..."

"You're kidding right?"

"No, I'm not," I handed him the plastic bag.

"Thanks," he was humouring me. I could tell he thought I was delusional.

"Come on Archie," I called Archie over to me – he was busy having fun with the two fierce dogs, apparently he'd come to an agreeable understanding with them.

We had to get away before the man looked in the bag and discovered the Scottish hundred-pound notes and started asking questions.

We ran from the Community Centre and shot out of sight round a corner and got a taxi all the way home and checked if our leopard was in the long grass. Nothing. No sign. But at least the wife beater Gauguin would soon be doing some good. Sometimes you just have to adjust your dreams to suit the circumstances.

It's been three months and our leopard has not returned.
Me and Archie have waited and waited and bit by bit our
hope is running out. We've got plenty of money, but
money doesn't bring you happiness and it can't make our
leopard come back.

"You're dying of boredom. What you waiting for,
anyway? Was it a good idea to give up your job?" my
mum said.

I bumped into my ex-boss. I pretended I didn't know
him – he's not the sort of person me and Archie mix
with, anymore.

My ex-boss has plenty of money and he looked very
well too – he prefers money to dreams and, maybe, he's
right about money. Money can buy food and clothes, and
fix the roof and draft-proof the door, and quite a few of
the homeless of Brixton aren't homeless because of the
Gauguin money.

My hair has grown back so I don't wear my
Swedish-blonde wig anymore and I've sold my new red
car and put the money in the bank – our days of flashy
driving are over. Archie sits around moping a lot of the
time and if we don't do something positive soon we'll
fade away into terminal inactivity.

So that's why me and Archie decided to set off in
search of our leopard again. This time we're going on
foot and searching in circles beginning with a circle
around the neighbourhood and on and on in ever-

increasing circles until we've covered the whole world. That's what I told Archie and he believes me.

We're also going to keep our ears and eyes and Archie's nose on the alert for any leopard related news – strange smells; chickens missing; more than usual big cat sightings; raids on supermarket bins.

So far we've talked to our neighbours and found out that the woman with the chickens has got more chickens and not one of them has been attacked, which is a sure sign our leopard hasn't been this way.

We widened our circle and came to the lane with the rabbits and the wood and made a diversion to look in the bins behind the supermarket. The diversion was Archie's idea – he loves bins and insists on following his nose but I've told him that, as the leader, it's me, not his nose, who chooses where we go.

Very early the next day, we crossed over the motorway on a foot bridge where some cows were crossing, and, even though Archie is eons away from being a wolf, they didn't believe it and ganged up on him, forcing him against the railings so I had to stand tall and shoo them away – which means I'm a hero in Archie's eyes. If our leopard was here, he'd try to eat one of those cows. We walked all day and were even more exhausted than the day before.

On the third day, I realised that the ever-increasing circles plan would only work if there were hundreds of people helping. I had to think of something else. Flying over the country at night in a helicopter with a heat seeking camera would be ideal – I might see our leopard's sleek form pouncing on a rabbit in a hedgerow – but that option is too expensive now I've given the one hundred thousand to the homeless of Brixton. So I've conceded that Archie was right in the first place – his nose is the best option and much cheaper than a helicopter. It'll probably mean going over old ground – neighbour's chickens, the lane with the rabbits, supermarket bins, that sort of thing, but there's a chance Archie can sniff out our leopard, if our leopard came back this way and then wandered off again...

I put on jeans and my blue jumper and packed two cheese and pickle sandwiches and two pairs of trainers into a backpack and put my phone, my credit card and three Scottish hundred-pound notes into my pocket – we were travelling light – I say *we*, Archie always travels light, that's one of the advantages of being a dog.

Just before we left, I phoned my mum. I told her we were off on our travels again and she said she was really worried about me and she'd been thinking a lot recently and thought that I should see someone. I told her I was fine. There was nothing to worry about and Archie was fine too.

And then she said, "Please don't go. If you go, I'm coming with you."

This would be disastrous because our leopard wouldn't come anywhere near us if my mum was there – she's a very formidable woman. I told her it definitely wasn't a good idea and she would hate it because we were *walking*. Once she'd heard we were walking, she changed her mind.

"Well then, if I'm not coming with you *must* phone me every day," she said.

"Definitely," I said. "We're leaving now."

"Good luck!" she called out as I switched off my phone.

"Find our leopard!" I told Archie. And, with that, me and Archie walked out of the house and into the back garden where Archie sniffed about in the long grass and set off at a pace. He headed straight up the road, down a garden path, round the house and to the woman's chicken pen where five chickens were scratching about. When they saw Archie, they panicked and threw themselves at the netting.

"Archie, come away. Now!" I dragged him away fast before the woman came out and called the police and put Archie in the frame for the original slaughter.

Hours later, we were in the lane with Archie chasing rabbits and not much sign of him tracking down our leopard. So we stopped and ate the two cheese and pickle sandwiches. Archie spat out the pickles.

After this Archie got more enthusiastic. He dived under hedges and across fields and skirted around towns until he sensed there was a supermarket bin nearby, then he made a run for it and when he got there hung around the bins looking hopeful – which made me think that perhaps he really was tracking down our leopard, who'd been here before us – but, on the other hand, made me think he wasn't tracking down our leopard at all and just wanted some more chicken legs.

It was midnight and Archie was leading me to another supermarket bin but this time when we got nearer Archie started to creep along and I heard it too. Sounds of something shuffling around inside the bin! Was it our leopard? We waited. We waited for a beautifully spotted form to leap out. We waited for a glimpse of greenish-golden eyes. Instead a red woolly hat with a miner's headlamp popped up.

"Hi there. Nothing worth having left in here," said a young man, as he climbed out of the bin with a packet of tomatoes in his hand. He put the packet of tomatoes into his backpack and switched off his headlamp. "Name's Freebird."

Evidently, he's a professional bin raider, working undercover. He took a muffin out of his back pack, unwrapped it and gave it to Archie. Archie now thinks he's wonderful.

"Do you come here often?" I was a bit stuck for words.

"Been coming here for a couple of years now. Went to a workshop in Wales; *How to make a good living from bins and be safe.* You should try it," he said.

"We're searching for a...a friend. We thought you were him."

"Homeless is he... your friend?" He unwrapped another muffin and handed it to me.

"Sort of." I ate the muffin. It had blueberries in it.

"It's my philosophy", he said," that, if we didn't waste so much food, the world would be a happier place. Now most people want food that's as fresh as possible but some people, take me for example, don't mind if the food's not that fresh...out of date by a day, say...or there's a banana that's a bit black but great inside...or a tomato that's a bit squashy...people like you and me don't care, and so supermarkets should give this food to people like us. But do they? No! No, they don't! And why not? Money. Money. Money. That's all they care about. They think they'll lose money if they give food to people like us. They think everyone will want out of date food and squashy bananas and tomatoes with spots. And will they? No, they won't! Because most people are picky or snobby or both, so it ends up with us, the unpicky, the unsnobbish, the penniless ones, being forced to get the food from bins but at least there's workshops. There were people in wheelchairs at the workshop, you know. We're fighting the inbuilt wastage of capitalism."

Freebird's got a lot to say for himself. He's got a point about inbuilt wastage though and I hope he doesn't meet up with our leopard one night when they're both out hunting.

"I'm off now to get some kip. Good luck with finding your friend." His round smiling face turned to Archie who was looking up at him adoringly and expecting another muffin.

Me and Archie watched him disappear into the night. He was whistling as he went which just goes to show that finding food in bins can bring great happiness.

*

Archie sat down and refused to go any further and I knew what he meant. We'd covered thirty miles and walked all night and only had two cheese and pickle sandwiches and two muffins to eat between us. The sun was just coming up over the Malvern Hills. I sat down next to Archie and watched the sun rise and before we knew it we were lying on the grass and falling asleep.

Sleeping in the Malvern hills in the late summer is ok if it doesn't rain. If it rains the best thing to do is make for the nearest Bed and Breakfast and hope they let you in, even if you look a mess. They didn't let us in.

After being rejected by the Bed and Breakfast, Archie decided to catch his own breakfast by chasing a rabbit down the hill.

"You don't stand a chance!" I shouted after him. I saw the rabbit disappear down a hole.

"Told you!"

*

Hours later, we were still walking and this time, instead of tracking down supermarket bins, Archie went from one rabbit hole to another – which could either mean our leopard had been here hunting rabbits and Archie was hot on his trail, or, Archie was determined to catch a rabbit and eat it for his breakfast.

At last we came to a cafe and sat outside and ordered two Full English Breakfasts from a skinny, nervous man, who ignored Archie and looked me up and down, warily.

Full English Breakfasts smack of unhealthy, olde-worlde food eaten by people who think there's no room for *foreigners* like me, but it's amazing what you'll eat if you're hungry. I gave all the sausages and bacon and a slice of toast to Archie and paid with one of my hundred-pound notes, which upset the man quite a lot and he said I should have asked whether they took hundred-pound Scottish notes *before* we ate the breakfast and I said, if I had then he would have said, no, and then me and Archie would have fainted with hunger and, anyway, there was nothing wrong with the money. It was real money – a gift from a Scottish relative. Then, he said I'd have to wait while his wife drove into town to the bank and checked it out and I said I couldn't wait and got up and left.

"Keep the change," I shouted over my shoulder, "On second thoughts give, it to charity." I bet they don't.

"I'm calling the police now!" I heard him shout when he realised we were leaving.

We could have been disheartened but it's amazing how good you feel after a Full English Breakfast, even if it's bad for you.

Archie seemed to know where he was heading now and, since I had no better ideas, I followed him. He was keeping to the wildest places, through woods, across fields, splashing along streams. We travelled for miles until my hair had bits of twigs sticking out of it, my jeans were torn and my trainers totally wet and still no sign of our leopard.

It was getting dark, when we saw a fence ahead of us. Archie stopped dead, sniffed the air and stared at it – all the hairs on his back were standing on end.

"What you staring at? It's not dangerous. It's just a fence," I told him.

Archie sat down and looked at me – he wasn't convinced – if dogs could talk, life would be much easier.

"Ok, I'll check it out for you," I said and strolled up to the fence, with a show of confidence, to impress Archie with my leadership skills. He stayed exactly where he was – he wasn't fooled – he knows when I'm nervous.

It was a chain link fence, at least five metres high with an overhang at the top and a few metres within this fence there was another and then a deep moat. Someone was keeping everyone out and something big in. I spotted a huge chunk of raw meat lying in the grass on the other side of the moat. So Archie's nose had led us to a chunk of meat – which was pretty typical of him.

Chain link fences, a moat, and raw meat, could only mean one thing. This was a remote corner of a wildlife park and there were probably lions lurking in the undergrowth ready to come back to their unfinished meal of half a horse. I backed away slowly and joined Archie at staring in the direction of the meat.

"You can't have that meat," I told him. "It's for the lions." I think Archie already knew this. He was hiding behind me – it's a good job he doesn't know my limitations.

Maybe, our leopard had been here too and smelled the meat but decided it was safer to catch a couple of rabbits instead. Maybe, our leopard once lived in this wildlife park or a wildlife park like this. If he did, was he happy? And, if we found him, would I still keep him a secret? Or, this time, would I report him to the RSPCA, or the zoo, or the police? – so that he could be returned to a safe life. Because, in a place like this, our leopard would have all the home comforts and it would be much safer for everybody and people would pay good money to appreciate his stunning beauty.

Except, his stunning beauty is mostly made up of his fierce independence, his wildness and his cunning, and, if I did report him, all that would be taken away.

Anyway, our leopard had rejected the comforts of captivity – he'd already chosen the freedom of life on the outside and preferred the challenge of raiding chicken coops and scavenging in supermarket bins. And, also, if we turned our leopard in, it could mean the end of my independence, my wildness and my cunning and Archie's too.

Except, me and Archie aren't really all that independent, or wild, or cunning – and living the wild life could turn out to be a bit of a letdown. For one thing, you still have to get organised, and even go on training courses on how to get food from bins and you have to go out hunting at night and, I wouldn't be surprised, if disputes broke out about who should be the first to rummage through the highest yielding bins. And then there's the fact that the whole of civilisation has struggled to get to the point where we don't have to be independent, or wild, or cunning – instead, we can relax, and lie back and not worry about a thing – and buy just whatever we want. But it hasn't worked out because, once you can relax and buy everything you want, you don't want this any more...you want something else...something wild and untamed...something...

Archie nudged me. Archie doesn't worry about the progress of civilisation. Food and friendship. Friendship and food. That's what really matters to him. Also, he doesn't like the dark when lions are about and I don't blame him. He leapt away across the field. I could see his pale shape bounding along in the distance.

He was waiting for me at the top of a motorway embankment. We kept walking for hours along the embankment until I was exhausted and Archie had stopped looking over his shoulder for lions out to eat us and decided it was safe and finally flopped down for a rest, just as it got light. This wasn't a good idea because, now it was light, we could easily be spotted on the embankment by any passing motorway patrol car.

I could see a motorway service station in the distance so we made for that. When we arrived, I took Archie in with me – I couldn't risk him being stolen and put up to ransom, because he looks like a pedigree, even though he isn't. It was very early in the morning and the place was empty and I thought I'd get away with having a dog with me.

"He a guide dog?" a man's voice called out, immediately.

I turned and saw it came from a middle-aged man serving behind the hot food counter.

"Yes, he's in training...except he's on his day off today."

"I believe you. Thousands wouldn't," he said.

The man was smiling so we went over to the counter where I bought fish and chips and a coffee.

"Could I have a bowl of water for him?"

"No problem," the man said. He had one of those encouraging faces you get in people who've lived their lives without ambition and one-upmanship.

We took our fish and chips outside and sat down at a bench. The man came out with the bowl of water and a sausage for Archie and made a great fuss of him. Sometimes dogs are higher up the social scale than I am – which is good news for Archie but bad news for the state of our society.

"If you had any spare money would you give it to a Dog's Home?" I asked the man.

"Oh yes, dogs aren't as much trouble as people," he said and gave Archie another pat on the head before he went back inside to his hot food counter.

He had a point. Even though dogs are another species, some people would rather help homeless dogs just because they are another species – people are much easier to dislike and more of a threat – people argue and fight over almost everything – like god or skin colour or even the clothes you wear. Whereas dogs are interested in two things – friendship and food. At least Archie is.

After our meal, I fell asleep on the bench and Archie fell asleep under it. We'd been asleep for hours before we were woken up by three coach-loads of pensioners who were laughing and joking and making the most of every moment they'd got left. Archie lives in the moment too – he doesn't care how long he's been here or how long he's got left, for that matter. Sometimes, I envy him that.

When one of the pensioners answered her phone, I remembered the promise to my mum.

"Hello, mum, sorry I haven't phoned."

"You switched your phone off! I was going to call the police. Where are you?"

"At a motorway service station."

"What are you doing there, for goodness sake?"

"Eating fish and chips and having a nap."

"I wish you'd come home."

"We're heading North...following Archie's nose."

"For goodness sake, that dog's got a lot to answer for!"

"He's ok. He seems to know where he's going." As soon as I'd said this, I knew I shouldn't have.

"That's it! Come home! You can't live your life following Archie's nose. He's taking you in the wrong direction. Please come home." I could tell she was getting desperate.

"I'm not really following Archie's nose. I'm really going to see a friend at the Laughing Horse pub in Scotland." As soon as I'd said this, I realised it wasn't such a bad idea. After all, if Archie was right, our leopard was heading that way, anyway.

"Do I know this friend?"

"No. He's called Graham. You'd like him. I've got to go now."

"Please be careful and phone tomorrow."

While I was on the phone, Archie was suddenly surrounded by some of the pensioners who stroked him and gave him biscuits and said how wonderful he was and, in the end, I had to drag him away and remind him that he was supposed to be tracking down our leopard. He trailed reluctantly behind me until he finally gave up on the pensioners. He's got a long memory and he's very stubborn at times. Once he was in the lead again, we went in circles until his nose pointed us in a northerly direction – I checked it was North on my phone and then had to switch it off quickly because *Connect to charger* popped up and I haven't got the charger with me, for one thing, and there's nowhere to plug one in, for another. If the battery goes dead and Archie's nose lets me down, I'll have to navigate by the sun or is it the North star?

We were in Cheshire again. Cheshire is flat and packed full of cows. Cows are supposed to be docile but these cows let out primeval bellows and turned into mobs of vengeful destruction as soon as they clapped eyes on Archie. They blame him for the deaths of their ancestors – it's a good job he can run fast.

Now, if we'd had our leopard with us, it would have been different – but there was still no sign of him.

*

I switched on my phone for a few seconds to check if we were still heading North. My feet were killing me – I'd already gone through one pair of trainers and had lots of blisters. I envy Archie – he doesn't have any trouble with his feet.

*

Once you start travelling the road opens up before you and time lengthens out, which is a good thing if you haven't got blisters. Time is one of those things that either slips through your fingers without you noticing or slogs along stolidly, just when you wish it wouldn't. Archie ignores time. I envy him that too.

*

Since we've reached the Lake District, Archie has been leaping into every lake we've passed. He's a great swimmer. First, he sniffs the shoreline and then he takes the plunge. Sometimes, I think I see our leopard swimming with Archie out there in the middle of the lake, but it turns out to be the ripple of a wave or the glint of the sunlight on the water. Sometimes, I imagine our leopard travelling far away to somewhere more suited to his wild beauty. Sometimes, I think we'll never see our leopard again.

But we keep going because, now, we don't know how to stop and, if we did stop, we'd always be thinking he was out there somewhere and we should have kept on searching until we'd found him.

*

Routine always set in after a while. It's called having structure in your life. Walk until dusk; find a pub; have a meal; stay the night and, if they says *No Dogs Allowed,* sneak Archie in when they're all asleep; get up at first light; have breakfast; phone mum; walk until dusk; find a pub; have a meal...

Archie leads the way – he's the one with the magnificent nose, except today Archie hasn't been in the lead at all.

"You're supposed to be showing *me* the way." I told him but he still lagged behind and sometimes stopped altogether and looked over his shoulder. Perhaps, he was remembering the pensioners, with regret, because he hadn't got his fair share of biscuits. Perhaps, he was remembering the time when our leopard had followed us.

We set off again with me in the lead but, now I was in the lead, it was obvious we weren't tracking our leopard any more. I stopped. It was hopeless. Even Archie had given up on the search and, maybe, he was right. Maybe, our leopard didn't want to be found and had been avoiding us all this time in case I captured him and put him in the leopard equivalent of a residential home for the elderly. He was independent, wild and cunning and he was going to stay that way.

We reached a lakeside and I began to get jumpy and the jumpier I got, the jumpier Archie got. Could it be a mad-axe murderer on our trail or the white haired black-eyebrowed man from the criminal underworld determined to get his money back because the Gauguin had turned out to be a fake. Or could it be the man from Brixton Community Centre determined to give the money back before he got thrown into prison for handling stolen money? I started running and kept turning round quickly to catch them out. That's the trouble with spending all your time with only a dog for company – you've got no one to tell you you're acting crazy.

I was wandering around the country in ever-decreasing circles. I was going over the same ground again and again and again...on foot...by car...on foot...north...south...east...west...again and again and again. And Archie came with me because he's my friend...and that's what friends do... I flopped to the ground, exhausted. Archie rushed up to me and licked my face. He lay by my side – I could tell he was worried about me. I was at a crossroads. Despair or hope? Give up the search or keep on trying? Mediocrity or miracle?

There was a tremendous splash. Archie gone for a swim in the lake? But, I realised he was still lying there, right beside me.

I jumped up. Circles of tiny waves moved outwards from the point where something big had dived. I looked at Archie – he was pretending to snooze now.

Gradually the waves disappeared. It could have been a very big fish leaping out to catch a fly.

"A very big fish," I told Archie.

I've noticed that, whenever I come to a conclusion about anything, there's always something that makes me think again and sends me in the opposite direction. Through the sun's glare I saw the magnificent sight of our leopard leaping through the water towards us. Beautiful spots shimmering. Greenish-golden eyes. A mirage and a daydream.

When his plate sized paws knocked me to the ground, I knew he was real. He was purring loudly and licking my face. I was so pleased to see him, I lost all my fear and stroked his head lovingly. He purred even louder and Archie began to bark. Our leopard turned and went over to him and their heads touched and our leopard stood tall and roared and showed his teeth and for a second I thought he was going to eat Archie on the spot but Archie was wagging his tail – so, either, he wasn't going to be eaten, or, he was going to be eaten and didn't mind.

Then our leopard leapt away and plunged into the lake again. I could see his head above the water. I turned and saw a man with a collie dog coming towards us.

"Morning," he said when he reached us.

"Morning," I said.

People round here don't say much.

Me and Archie waited for the man and the collie to disappear down the hill before we ran to the water's edge. Archie leapt in and swam after our leopard who was almost out of sight.

Our leopard's more than a powerful swimmer – he's definitely the sort of leopard who can look after himself. He'd lived off the fat of the land for more than three months. Cities, suburbia, the countryside – these were his hunting grounds – he raided supermarket bins; he caught rabbits hiding in hedgerows; he ate chickens out of back gardens. He hunted with stealth under the cover of darkness and his beautiful spots were the perfect camouflage in the tree tops as he slept the days away. And, so far, he hadn't eaten any people, well, not that I'd heard about. He's a solitary leopard and I don't think he likes people much – only me, he likes me, when he first saw me, from the long grass in my back garden, he knew he could trust me. And he likes Archie, of course, but then Archie's a very likeable dog.

Suddenly Archie was swimming back towards the shore and swimming fast after him was our leopard. Archie splashed out covering me with water. Our leopard leapt out and threw a fish down at my feet.

First a Gauguin and now a fish. What else could you ask for? The fish flopped about and I felt sorry for it but I didn't dare throw it back in case our leopard took offence. Our leopard had his eye on the fish and then with one slap of his paw he killed it stone dead – never take liberties with leopards – leopard's don't understand the concept of vegetarianism. I'm not really a vegetarian

– I eat fish that other people have killed for me, which makes me a hypocrite.

Our leopard was staring at me with his greenish-golden eyes. He isn't a creature of these islands – he belongs in exotic places but somehow has ended up here, on a rainy grey island – he's a foreigner, like me.

Archie barked at the fish. He was trying to decide if it was safe to eat it. If he did, would our leopard pounce on him for eating a fish that was given to me?

"Leave!" I told Archie, just in case he risked it.

Now the fish was dead, our leopard lost interest in it and strolled away to the nearest tree. He climbed to a high branch where he draped himself languidly over it. We could hear him purring from where we stood.

Archie started barking.

"Afternoon" It was the man with the collie again.

"Afternoon."

"That's a big fish you've got there. You catch it?"

"No, my dog."

Just when you want people *not* to talk to you, they do. The man started talking about the fish, and all the time I was thinking that I couldn't hear our leopard purring, which probably meant he was about to leap down the tree and, if I was lucky, he'd only eat the collie and leave the man whole.

The man spent ages giving me instructions on how to gut a fish and even handed me some matches so I could make a camp fire and cook the fish because, he said, although it was probably illegal to get fish from these waters, it was a shame to waste it and, he confided in me, he wouldn't mind having a clever dog like that himself because it would definitely save on the food bills.

"Nice talking to you," he said, finally going on his way.

"You too," I sighed with relief and our leopard started purring again.

I looked at the fish. There was no chance I was going to gut it but I could cook it whole and give the disgusting bits to Archie. Archie doesn't suffer from disgust. I don't envy him that.

While our leopard slept, me and Archie collected twigs and branches and built a fire. I arranged the wood into a wigwam shape – tiny twigs first, then small twigs, then bits of branches. Archie thought it was a game and kept running off with the largest branches until I set fire to the wigwam and then he sat down and, together, we watched the flames until the fire burnt down to glowing embers. I put the fish on top of the embers flipping it over with a stick.

I ate the white bits, Archie ate the skin and everything else. He particularly liked the disgusting bits.

We lay on the grass and relaxed. We felt we deserved it. We'd found our leopard – well our leopard had found us; we'd helped the Homeless of Brixton; and the only thing left to do was to escape to Africa with our leopard. And now we'd got to this crucial part of our plan, I began to consider it in the light of common sense.

The light of common sense can often lead you to conclude that life is meant to be dull and safe and the only feasible way forward is to get on with it and make the best of it and accept the everyday mundanity.

According to common sense, going to Africa didn't make any sense at all.

For one thing, Archie would hate the long journey so I'd have to leave him behind. But he could stay with my mum. He's always happy when he's with her because she has a routine of eating biscuits and cakes everyday and she lets him sleep on her settee. He'd probably miss me, but the biscuits and cakes would make up for it.

Our leopard would be the main problem. Even if I managed to get him on board a plane, disguised as an oversized rare breed of domestic cat, or, as a circus animal about to perform in a star-studded show, even if I managed this – and it would cost a lot and I'd have to bribe a few people – even if I managed this, now I thought about it, once he got to Africa, he might feel out of place there, now that he'd made a life for himself here.

I decided to keep going North to Scotland where our leopard could hide in the forest and eat deer. Me and Archie could go to the Laughing Horse and eat fish and chips and beef sandwiches and ask Graham for advice. I looked down at Archie. He wagged his tail lazily – he's not prone to thinking too much.

*

The following day the three of us carried on northwards towards Graham and the Laughing Horse. We crossed fells, avoided hills and strolled along lakesides. During the day, our leopard slept up trees and there was no way he was going to come down so we walked on without him. The first day, we walked only a little way ahead and hid behind a rock to test if he could find us. And that evening he tried to creep up on us but Archie's not easy to creep up on and ran up to him barking. Our leopard welcomed him with a tap of his paw which knocked Archie right off his feet. I sympathised with Archie – I know what a gentle tap from a leopard's paw feels like.

After that first day, we travelled further and further from our leopard while he slept up a tree and every evening our leopard caught up with us and, as soon as it was dark, he'd go off hunting and, in the morning, we'd find a fish at our feet. When he threw the fish at my feet, I stroked his head and he purred but I didn't trust him entirely and neither did Archie. His claws and teeth are too big. He could easily eat us.

We were getting better at cooking fish and didn't visit cafes much now because there was a chance our leopard might come down from the tree he'd chosen to sleep in, follow us to the cafe and raid the kitchen.

And there was another reason we didn't visit cafes as much. We smelt bad. Well, Archie always smells pretty bad, whereas I don't, but living rough soon makes you smell and look like a dodgy character. But at least I got my phone charged up at the last cafe. The owner took pity on me and lent me a charger and let me use her electricity. It's called the kindness of strangers.

I needed a shower. I'd tried swimming in my underwear but it's a risky business. If anyone sees me they might report me for unsettling the symmetry of the landscape – I'll be glad when we get to the Laughing Horse.

*

We'd been through countryside dotted with sheep
and I was worrying what I'd do if our leopard brought
me a dead sheep as a present. It'd been fish up to now but
what happens when we leave the lakes and rivers
behind?

I found out the next day when I woke up under the
hedge where me and Archie were sheltering for the
night. A dead rabbit lay next to me. I don't eat rabbits.
Archie does, but I wouldn't let him have it until we'd
built a fire and roasted it, because I didn't want Archie
turning into a wild beast with blood dripping from his
fangs.

The day after that our leopard brought me a half
eaten pizza so I guess he'd made a foray into the nearest
town, which was very worrying.

Now I'd got my phone on again, I kept getting calls
and texts from my mum. I told her that me and Archie
were fine and we'd had a bit of luck and found a friend.
She asked what I meant by *found* and I said it was more
that we bumped into him and he was going the same way
as us so we were travelling together, so she needn't
worry because he was big and strong and wouldn't take
any nonsense from anybody.

She asked me if she knew this friend and I told her
that she didn't but I was sure she'd like him if she met
him.

We found a deserted beach today. Archie and our
leopard went for a swim while I sat on the beach keeping
a lookout. I was beginning to feel it was only a matter of

time before our leopard was discovered and, the longer he stayed close to us, the more likely this became. A sense of foreboding settled over me and I remembered what the old woman in Glasgow had said about it all ending badly. Archie and our leopard were splashing about out there full of joy. They don't care about the future – I let the future taint the present because I know it can all end badly and the chances of it ending well are...I heard voices behind me.

"Archie! Archie!" I called out. Archie ignored me – probably because he doesn't care about the future, which turned out to be a good thing because the voices belonged to an old couple who smiled at Archie swimming out there and just walked straight on by – if Archie had come back to me, maybe our leopard would have swum closer to the shore too and the old couple would've seen our leopard clearly and it would all have ended badly, there and then.

Our leopard was so far out, if they spotted him now they'd think he was a seal or the light playing on the sea. They'd never know it was our leopard powering his way through the waves.

*

At last we were heading down the road leading to the Laughing Horse. Our leopard was asleep in the oak tree in the wood. He'd been out all night hunting rabbits – I knew because he'd given me a rabbit for my breakfast. I carried it by its legs and felt sorry that it'd been killed on my account and the least I could do was give it to Graham who could give it to Ashar, the Middle

127

Eastern cook, who probably knew how to make something tasty with it.

Graham was sitting behind the empty bar reading a book when we went in, "Wow! It's you! You look..."

"Dirty and smelly. You needn't be polite," I said.

"Great to see you both," Archie was jumping all over him in excitement. "What can I get you?"

"A shower and fish and chips and a beer and a beef sandwich for Archie...oh and I've got a present for you." I handed him the rabbit, "I'm a vegetarian – except I eat fish."

"Where'd you get it?" he looked at it carefully.

"A friend caught it for me," I said.

"This friend of yours, doesn't know you very well then, does he," he said.

"He doesn't understand vegetarianism, that's all." I sounded a bit defensive.

Graham smiled, "I'll give it to Ashar. Maybe he'll make a stew or something and, if you really do want a shower, you can use the bathroom..."

"Thank you! Thank you! Thank you!" Living off the fat of the land makes you appreciate people who share their bathroom.

"Top of the stairs on the right..."

I was up the stairs before he'd finished speaking. Archie stayed by his side – he knows when there's a beef sandwich nearby.

I pulled off my clothes and jumped in the shower. I washed myself again and again until my skin glowed and my hair was squeaky clean. I looked at my filthy clothes. There was no way I was going to put them on like that. I got to work washing them.

"How long you going to be in there!" Graham shouted through the door.

"A minute...or two," I rinsed the clothes and wrapped them in a towel and wrapped the other towel round myself and stepped out of the bathroom to go downstairs.

Graham saw me at the top of the stairs. He came up the stairs, followed by Archie, and went into a bedroom, followed by Archie, and came out with a shirt and a pair of shorts, followed by Archie – obviously Archie hadn't had his beef sandwich yet, "You can wear these for now," Graham smiled.

I went back into the bathroom and made myself presentable by rolling up the sleeves of the shirt and turning down the collar. I rolled up the legs of the shorts and tucked the shirt into the shorts so I looked stylishly casual and went downstairs.

The same three men were now at the bar. This time they all smiled, even the one who hates foreigners. It's called familiarity breeding a reluctant acceptance – as long as they don't have to see me in here too often.

I sat down at our table and soon there was my fish and chips and beer and Archie had his beef sandwich and we were the picture of happiness. Living of the fat of the land makes you appreciate the refinements of civilisation.

"Last time you were here, we saw a big cat," the leery red-faced one shouted over to me.

"Some woman with a screw loose started spreading rumours about seeing a leopard – believed her, they did, but we *saw* one and nobody believed us. Said we were drunk," the old bald man said, bitterly.

129

"Well we were drunk," the middle aged man with the grey hair said.

They went on like this while I was thinking that our leopard may have woken up and be waiting in the car park ready to pounce on them when they left.

When Graham came over to clear our table I said, "I need your advice, urgently."

He sat down and looked at me cautiously, "What about?" He's very suspicious – he knows I'm the leopard hoaxer, I thought.

"I've got a friend who needs a place where he'll be safe," I whispered.

"Same friend who caught the rabbit?"

"Yes."

"Is he a criminal?"

"No, he's a..." I hesitated, should I tell Graham about our leopard? That our leopard was always in danger of being captured and that's why I spread the rumours and now I didn't know what to do next. I decided not to tell him – not yet anyway. "He's just a bit shy, that's all, I said."

"Are you sure *he's* not a *she*?"Graham said.

"You think I'm talking about myself? I can't catch rabbits!"

"Archie can," Graham said. Archie wagged his tail – he always does this when his name's mentioned.

"I'm not talking about myself!"

"Depends what you mean by safe and safe from what?"

"From people."

"So he *is* a criminal! You'd better be careful. He might be dangerous *if* he exists."

"I've told you! I'm not talking about myself and for your information, he is dangerous!" I was getting annoyed and giving too much away.

"That settles it. Call the police. Assisting an offender is a crime you know!" Graham was getting agitated.

"He's only dangerous to rabbits," I said quickly. I realised it was no use talking to Graham about our leopard. I changed the subject. "I think I worry too much about him. He's probably been eating too many rabbits," I laughed. "He'll be fine. I'll phone him later. How's business?"

"You're changing the subject," Graham said, "Are you sure this person isn't dangerous?"

"Absolutely positive," I lied, convincingly. "I've told you. I'll phone him later. He's probably gone travelling and doesn't need my advice anyway...so how is business?"

"Quiet. I like it quiet. Gives me time to read. As long as I can pay the bills..."

*

Graham is good looking, intelligent, and kind to Archie, but, I now realise, I can't tell him about our leopard. Our leopard belongs to me and Archie, alone.

*

Graham said I could sleep in the spare room, if I had nowhere else to stay, and Archie was welcome too, of course. I accepted immediately because I like Graham and because living off the fat of the land is overrated especially if the supplies of fish dry up and you don't eat rabbit.

I went up to the spare room early and spread all my wet clothes out to dry, lay on the bed and fell asleep immediately. Later on, I heard Graham let Archie into the room.

I was woken in the middle of the night by the sound of someone sawing wood. Our leopard! I jumped out of bed, put on Graham's shirt and shorts and whispered to Archie, "Follow me."

We crept downstairs and out of the front door and saw the shadowy outline of our leopard. He was roaring and standing over something large. He'd made a kill just for us. This was it all ending badly just as the old woman had warned. Our leopard would have to be shot.

I crept closer and our leopard began to purr. He was pleased with his gift and happy to see us. I hoped that, if it was one of the three men who propped up the bar, it was the old bald one with no teeth.

Archie was wagging his tail, which could mean that he was glad it was the old bald one with no teeth or...

I saw the shadowy form between our leopard's legs move. Whatever it was, it wasn't quite dead yet!

I heard a sound behind me and turned to see Graham silhouetted in the doorway.

"What's going on?" Graham called out.

Our leopard disappeared into the darkness.

"There's something dead or nearly dead out here," my voice sounded weak.

Archie ran up to the shape on the ground and a sheep scrambled to its feet and ran away. A sheep. Cats bring you live mice. Leopards bring you live sheep.

132

Graham was by my side now, "There's nothing here. You must have been dreaming or ..."

"Yes, a bad dream", I said, cheerfully – I was so happy the old bald man with no teeth hadn't been attacked by our leopard – and, when I thought about it, our leopard wouldn't have brought me such a disgusting present anyway.

We went back into the Laughing Horse and Graham made a hot milky chocolate drink and we had biscuits with it, which pleased Archie no end.

We went to bed just as it was getting light and I hoped our leopard would be sound asleep up a tree and not stalking sheep.

When we woke at midday, I knew that if our leopard had started catching sheep then it was definitely time to report him to the authorities. But he wasn't actually *eating* the sheep, as far as I knew, and he'd only brought me *one* live sheep as a present – so I decided not to act just yet. Sometimes inaction leads to the problem getting worse and worse and escalating into something insolvable. Sometimes inaction leads to time passing which leads to the problem evaporating because something crops up which solves the problem for you.

Graham took the day off and the three of us wandered around the countryside together and Graham told me how he used to work in the City of London and he'd made a packet and given it all up and bought the Laughing Horse because he liked the name and he liked the location. He thought it was beautiful round here – the only drawback was that some of the people were bigots of one sort or another but most were just ordinary types quietly living out their lives without ambition which he found refreshing.

I told him that I used to work in advertising – which was very well paid and great if you thought all your best ideas should be used to get innocent people to buy things they didn't need or even want and also it was all about cutting each other's throats and Daisy was after my job and had finally got it when I resigned, but not before I got a packet from the boss, who was glad to get rid of me in the end. And now I was wandering around the countryside with my friends.

"Friends?"

"I meant friend. Me and Archie."

"He is a great dog, isn't he," Archie wagged his tail. He loves Graham.

And I like Graham too. He's the sort of person I could be happy with but I have our leopard to consider. He might turn up with a live sheep tonight and stand outside roaring like someone sawing wood.

That night, I left the window open and waited for the roar of our leopard. Archie was snoring and I must have fallen into a deep sleep because the next thing I knew I was being nudged awake by Archie and I realised there was the unmistakeable sound of our leopard purring nearby.

I turned to the open window. Greenish-golden eyes stared at me and he had a pheasant in his mouth. I was so relieved that he hadn't brought me a sheep.

"Good leopard," I stroked his beautiful spotted head and took the pheasant gently from him. The pheasant was alive and, as soon as I put it down, it started flying all round the room and Archie started to chase it and bark and I shouted, "Stop it! Stop it!" which of course woke up Graham who came rushing into the room.

"Now what's going on!" he shouted.

Would he spot our leopard who was still balancing precariously on the window sill? I stood with my back to the open window. The purring had stopped but I could feel our leopard breathing down my neck. I hope he doesn't decide to take a friendly swipe at me, I thought.

Then I heard a thud as our leopard leapt away into the night.

Meanwhile Graham had caught the pheasant, "Got in through the window. Didn't know they could do that. We could eat it tomorrow."

"I'm a vegetarian," I said.

Archie was still leaping around and trying to take a bite out of the pheasant.

"Archie isn't," Graham said.

"Give it to me. It's my pheasant," I held out my hands.

"How d'you work that out?" Graham smiled.

"It was given to me...I mean it came through my window...."

"You're forgetting this is my spare room." But he passed the pheasant to me anyway and I went over to the window and threw it into the air and it fluttered and squawked and I wondered if our leopard would catch it again and eat it, this time.

"Let's get some sleep" Graham said holding me close and I went with him to his room but we didn't do much sleeping.

Being with Graham made my life even more complicated mostly because I'd got used to living on the edge with Archie and our leopard, and so adjusting to a quiet life, with a lovely man in a deserted pub, was not as easy as it should have been. It wasn't just that I missed the open road and the fish cooked on an open fire – and sometimes I even missed getting food out of supermarket bins– I also had to think about Graham as well now and I was still worrying about our leopard and how to get him to Africa and I lay awake half the night listening out for him.

A whole week went by and there were no more presents delivered in the middle of the night so I told Graham I was going for a walk in the dark with Archie. And Graham said he'd come with me but I said, no, we can't go everywhere together and, he said, he always had the feeling I was keeping something back from him and, I said, every couple has to let each other have a life of their own sometimes and he agreed and said, of course, but he still worried about me being out in the dark. But I've got Archie, I told him and, he said, you're right, see you later. So off me and Archie went in search of our leopard and he soon found us and brought me a present of a dead rabbit. I think he was going to eat it himself before he bumped into me and Archie.

We were so happy to see each other. I'd been missing our leopard's wildness and his greenish-golden eyes which seem to be getting fiercer – it's something that's difficult to give up, even if the man is lovely and the living easy.

Easy living. Archie likes easy living – friendship and food, punctuated with bursts of fun – chasing rabbits; playing football with Graham. I envy Archie sometimes.

My mum approves. Graham sent her a photo of us and she said we looked very happy together and at last I'd got someone to look after me, so she needn't worry any more. I told her I didn't need anyone to look after me, on the contrary.

Does our leopard need someone to look after him or not? He's a large carnivore on a small island and, if he stays around here any longer, he's going to get caught for sure. He should keep on the move to be safe but he stays here because me and Archie are here and, he is our friend, after all. He has choices, I suppose, but does he know that? Is it up to me to show him the way?

Choices. I asked Graham about choices and he looked fearful and said, if I didn't want to stay with him that was ok because you can't keep people if they don't want to stay, and, if you did manage to keep them by some form of deviousness, it never worked out, and I could go if I wanted to and if I wanted to come back at any time that would be good.

He doesn't know about our leopard and the danger our leopard's in and I can't tell him because our leopard will always be my and Archie's secret. He came to my back garden and he's our leopard. Except he isn't really *our* leopard...he's our secret friend and we don't own him.

Sometimes it's best to make a decision and get on with it because, if you don't, you don't get on with anything. Sometimes it's best not to make a decision because, if you do, you could be stuck with it, forever.

Me and Archie have taken to going out for very long walks while Graham stays behind the bar – he misses me but I have to think about our leopard and keep him out of harm's way.

We walked for miles one day until we reached the forest and it grew dark and we waited and in the middle of the night our leopard appeared. He'd brought me a dead mouse. I looked into his greenish-golden eyes and he stared back ferociously and I began to fear that soon I would be eaten by our leopard and Archie wouldn't be able to save me.

During the day I've been helping out with the cooking. Ashar, the Middle Eastern cook, has been complaining about always cooking fish and chips and says it's boring and, I said, well then, why not cook some Middle Eastern food one day a week and then maybe the locals will try it and like it and I could advertise it for him and you never know tourists might come and it could get quite popular and then he could ask Graham for a pay rise.

So, the first week, I made some posters and stuck them around the place, and Ashar stuffed cabbage leaves with rice, lamb, pine nuts and spices and stewed them in oil and tomato and he made some without the meat just for me and baked his own pitta bread – and it was delicious but none of the locals tried it and there were no tourists about (Archie loved the pitta bread).

The next week, Ashar mashed up some fava beans and served them with olive oil, parsley, onion, garlic and lemon juice and we served it with pitta bread, as a free taster, and a few of the locals tried it and one tourist, who'd seen one of my posters on a tree, came along and said it was very good.

The week after, I splashed out on the advertising and Ashar made a two course meal of mashed up fava beans to start and stuffed cabbage leaves as the main course. And there was a side dish of yoghurt mixed with pomegranate seeds, onions and coriander. Ashar said the diners could dip the pitta bread in the yogurt. Twenty people turned up and it was a great hit mostly because people dipped their chips in the yoghurt mix. Ashar said they needed educating.

Then Ashar asked Graham for a pay rise and he got it. Archie thinks the extra visitors are great, mostly because they give him chips and pieces of pitta bread.

I'd been listening out for our leopard every night but there was no sign of him. He was probably being more careful now more and more people were stopping off at the Laughing Horse to eat Ashar's meals.

Graham said that the Laughing Horse was getting known as one of the best places to eat around here thanks to Ashar's food and my advertising campaign and we made a good team and soon he'd have some spare cash even after Ashar's rise.

*

I hadn't seen our leopard for three weeks so I decided to go out and look for him.

"Me and Archie are just going out" I said as I walked past Graham who was serving at the bar.

"Look after her Archie!"Graham shouted after us.

We walked to the wood up the road and looked up into the branches of every tree. Our leopard is difficult to spot but Archie soon sniffed him out. He was draped over a branch looking down at us. He began to purr but stayed where he was until darkness fell, then he leapt down and bounded away towards the sea without a backward glance. Perhaps he was going sea fishing and he'd bring me back a cod.

I didn't get a cod or any other kind of fish or any kind of present live or dead for the next few weeks, which does have its advantages because it means you don't have to make up lies about how you came by it. But, nevertheless, I was disappointed – when you have a leopard bringing you presents, you're special. I'm sure Archie would agree with me, if he could talk.

Life at the Laughing Horse is pleasant except for the occasional bigot but I can deal with that with Archie and Graham on my side.

"Is it better to live a pleasant life or a life of heartache and ecstasy?" I asked Graham.

"Most people don't have to choose one or the other," he said.

"But choose one anyway," I said.

"If the life of heartache and ecstasy meant keeping someone I love even for a little while, I'd choose the heartache and ecstasy," he said.

That's the thing about Graham, he's always thinking about me – he's a bit like Archie except food's not quite as important to him.

*

The sound of sawing below our window! I had to act quickly before Graham woke up. I crept out of the bedroom, met Archie in the hallway and we snuck out into the night.

As our leopard came towards us, we could see he was carrying something. At last he was bringing me another present!

"Another present," I whispered to Archie.

Our leopard placed the present gently on my bare feet where I could feel its soft warmth. It was a black and white lamb.

"Thank you," I stroked our leopard and he began to purr and, as he turned and walked away, he was still purring. And there was something in the way he did it that made me cry and Archie whimpered too because he knew I was sad.

Our leopard had given me: a Gauguin, fish, rabbits, a half eaten pizza, a pheasant, a whole live sheep, a dead mouse, and now a lamb. Symbols of his friendship. And, of all his presents, I loved this lamb the best – even though the sale of the Gauguin was helping the homeless of Brixton.

"What are you two doing out here?" Graham was suddenly behind me.

"We've been given...we've found a lamb," I sniffed.

"Why are you crying? Is it dead?" he said.

"No," I started to sob, "it's...it's...so wonderful."

He held me close, "Well, yes, it is cute. Let's take it inside and have a look at it."

So we went inside and Graham made me a hot drink and, when at last I'd stopped sobbing, we had a good look at the lamb. It'd snuggled up to Archie who was giving it shifty sideways glances.

"It's a lamb of many colours. A Jacob lamb. Better than a Gauguin," I said.

"You really like Gauguin," Graham said.

"No, not really," I said, "he was a wife beater...his paintings aren't bad though."

"We'll have to find out where it came from and give it back."

"But I'd like to keep it."

"If no one claims it, I suppose we could. I'll put it in the garden for now," Graham picked up the lamb.

"No! No! It may escape...and get run over!" Or eaten by our leopard, I thought.

"Ok, I'll put it in the shed," Graham went out to the shed with the lamb in his arms.

*

I made up a few posters about the lost lamb and stuck one on the pub door and some on tree trunks but nobody came forward to claim it.

Ashar said it was about ten weeks old and we should feed it up and slaughter it and make lots of delicious meals with it and I told him that the lamb was mine and he was definitely *not* going to make meals out of it.

The lamb's a ewe and Graham said we should give it a name but I just call it our lamb and I think that's fine. It's already eaten most of the grass in the garden so now me and Archie take it on walks with us – it grazes by the

142

roadside and sometimes Archie grazes with it to show solidarity, which proves he thinks it's one of us now. We only take it for walks in the middle of the day when we're pretty sure our leopard is asleep.

*

Me and Archie weren't expecting to see our leopard any time soon but one moonlit night we heard the sound of sawing.

"Who's that sawing wood at this time of night?" Graham turned over in bed.

"Stay where you are, I'll check." I threw on some clothes and my trainers.

Me and Archie stepped out of the Laughing Horse and there was our leopard waiting. He stopped roaring when he saw us and turned and walked away and we followed him across the road and down the lane and across the fields and I fell in a stream but Archie jumped straight over it. Our leopard looked marvellous in the moonlight with his beautiful spots moving through the long grasses and finally his outline at the top of the sand dunes before he disappeared over them with Archie not far behind.

I ran after them and when I reached the top I looked down to the beach and saw Archie standing by the water's edge and saw our leopard already swimming out to sea.

I ran down the beach and stood by Archie and we watched together as our leopard swam further and further away from us. When he turned and looked back towards the shore, for a moment, I believed he was going to catch a fish for me and come back to us purring, carrying it in his mouth. But he went on swimming. He was swimming away from us. He was independent, wild and cunning and he was going to stay that way.

Although I knew it was pointless, I called out after him, "Don't leave. I don't want you to leave. We're supposed to be going to Africa together!"

And, now, I understood that he'd tried to tempt me with the lamb, his last and best present. But I had chosen Graham and easy living and delicious Middle Eastern food.

Me and Archie thought we could still see our leopard's head far away out there at sea and hoped he knew what he was doing and would find a quiet beach along the coast where he could rest and then maybe swim on to an island where he could hunt rabbits for a while before moving on.

We sat on the sand in a cloud of loss and I remembered the day I first saw him in the long grass in my back garden. His greenish-golden eyes and his beautiful spots.

Eventually we dragged ourselves back to the Laughing Horse and, as we walked, I tried to be happy for our leopard because, after all, he'd made a choice and I'd made mine. And, by the time we'd got to the Laughing Horse, a feeling of elation was replacing the sadness, because our leopard was out there living his life and who knows where he might end up. Africa?

I crept upstairs and slipped back into bed beside Graham.

"Who was it?" he mumbled.

"No one you knew," I said.

I couldn't sleep. I wondered how far our leopard had swum and how far leopards could swim before they got exhausted and drowned. But our leopard had a lot of sense and, if any leopard could survive out at sea, it was our leopard – Archie would definitely agree.

I tossed and turned with images of our leopard reaching exotic shores and, just as it was getting light, I got up and took Archie for a walk.

"Our leopard is the silver apples of the moon, the golden apples of the sun. He's tiger tiger burning bright in the forests of the night. He is such stuff as dreams are made on..." I told Archie. Archie doesn't understand poetry but he wagged his tail, anyway.

"...And he's our leopard – and since meeting him, we've learnt how to sleep under hedges and eat well from supermarket bins. And I've sold a Gauguin and helped the homeless of Brixton. And that's not all. We met Freebird, the fulfilled bin raider, and, best of all, we met Graham," Archie barked at the mention of Graham's name. Archie understands friendship better than anyone.

"I've worn wigs and had my car cleaned, until it was like-new, in Govan. We've eaten curry in Glasgow and I wore a red dress in a red car and you wore a red collar." Archie was still wagging his tail because he liked the sound of my voice and didn't know I was talking about the wigs and the collar which he hated.

"We've travelled up and down the country and met happy pensioners and miserable Bed and Breakfast owners and a leopard rescued by a gentle man, bearing beef. You remember the beef don't you?" I patted Archie's soft warm head. "But I still want more – just like our leopard, who couldn't rest from travel and roamed with a hungry heart." Archie was looking up at me. He'll miss me when I go.

Graham was cooking breakfast when we got back.

"You were up early," he said.

"Couldn't sleep. I was thinking about our..."

"Our plans for the future?" He sounded fearful.

"Well, yes, I suppose I was in a way."

"What way is that?" he asked.

"Well, you know how I planned to go to Africa."

"You still want to go then?"

"Well, yes, I suppose I do, but I don't want to leave you...Archie would be ok with my mum."

"You know I can't leave this place. Thanks to you and to Ashar's food, it's doing well and I like it here. Are you sure you want to leave?" Graham looked sad.

"But I'll be back!" I'd made up my mind, "I'll be back in six months."

"Six months! Think about it. Talk it over with your mum first. Don't do anything rash."

*

I thought about it.

What was so special about Africa? Well, for a start, that's where leopards live and where our leopard might be heading and that's where my ancestors came from. And it's a big and exciting place with deserts and jungle and grasslands. It has the Sahara, the Congo and the grasslands of Kenya.

But it's very wild and I wouldn't have Archie by my side because I couldn't risk him being eaten by a lion.

146

Instead, he'd be eating biscuits and sitting on my mum's settee and I would really miss him.

*

I phoned my mum.

"Can you look after Archie for a while?"

"How long?"

"Six months."

"Six months! Why six months?"

"I'm planning to explore Africa, especially Kenya where the tall grasses are."

"Tall grasses? It's dangerous there! You might get eaten by a lion! Is Graham going with you?"

"No. He's got to stay here."

"For goodness sake, you can't go on your own! I thought you were happy with Graham?"

"I am it's just...well it's just...I had a plan, a dream and I don't want to give up on it. A friend of mine. He's already gone."

"Why didn't you go with him?"

"He went by sea."

"All the way to Africa?"

"I'm not sure where he's heading first. He'll probably stop off in Ireland or Tenerife."

"Sensible friend. At least he'll see the sun in Tenerife. The weather's terrible here."

"So can you look after Archie?"

"Can't Graham look after him?"

"He would, if I asked, but, you know, you usually look after Archie and Graham's got our lamb to look after."

"Lamb?"

"I told you about our lamb. She was a present from the same friend. Remember?"

"This friend of yours has a lot to answer for. I'd like to give him a piece of my mind..."

"So will you look after Archie?"

"Yes, but I'm not happy with you going away and I'll only look after him if I can come and stay up there."

When we got back to the Laughing Horse, I found Graham, sitting behind the bar, drinking whisky and looking miserable.

"You're drinking whisky," I said.

He nodded, "Best malt."

"You don't like whisky," I said.

"I know," he said.

"I've spoken to my mum and she wants to come and stay up here while I'm away and help you look after Archie."

"Stay up here? With Archie? So you're coming back." He stood up and put the whisky bottle back on the shelf.

*

It didn't take long to get things organised. My mum came to stay the very next day – I think she was having some relationship problems and wanted to escape for a while. She gets on well with Ashar. They're about the same age and Graham says there's a romance brewing. They argue a bit over food but, now, every Wednesday, they cook Caribbean food, which is proving just as popular as the Middle Eastern.

Archie is going to miss me but he's loving all the extra attention from my mum and has formed a bond with our lamb – probably because our lamb likes eating grass and not biscuits – Archie's very competitive when it comes to biscuit eating.

I've been putting the leftover Gauguin money into the bank, bit by bit, and should have enough to set up a leopard sanctuary in Africa.

I've booked my tickets and packed a few clothes and I've got my credit card and my bank card and my phone, which probably won't work over there.

*

I said goodbye to my mum and Ashar and Archie and our lamb and told them I'll be back soon.

Graham drove me to the airport and we both cried but we know this is something I have to do – because if you have dreams and you don't at least try to fulfil them, you're never the same again, and I know Archie and our leopard would agree with me.

Our leopard has probably already reached the west coast of Ireland where he's resting and catching a few fish before he swims off to Portugal. From Portugal, it's a long swim to the Canary islands but once he's there, I bet, he'll find a deserted beach and warm himself on the black volcanic sands and, then, he'll swim across to Senegal where he'll have to be careful of the crocodiles, if he swims in the rivers.

*

After months of crossing Africa, our leopard will climb to the grassland heights of Kenya, where he'll find

149

a tree and his limbs will hang languidly over a branch
and his greenish-golden eyes will close and his beautiful
spots will keep him safely hidden from the lions, as he
sleeps the day away in the leafy shadows.

Also by Sue Bates

A series of humorous, illustrated, books for 5 to 8 year
olds: *The Bold Worm*; *The Independent Ant*; *The Lazy Bee*;
The Flying Caterpillar; and *The Carefree Ladybug*.

Supersleuths in Space aka Intergalactic Posties,
a novel for 8 to 11 year olds.

Penny Whistle the Bread Bin Mouse,
a limited edition book for 5 to 8 year olds.

What is a Watt? The Adventures of Five Light Bulbs,
an educational, humorous, illustrated book
for 5 to 8 year olds.

Little Old Lady, a novel following the adventures of a
woman determined to escape the confines of old age.

www.bothy-publishing.com
enquiries@bothy-publishing.com